LAWFULLY DEFENDED

BOOKS BY ELLE E. KAY

FAITH WRITES PUBLISHING

Endless Mountain Series:

Shadowing Stella
Implicating Claudia
Chasing Sofie

The Lawkeepers Series:
CONTEMPORARY LAWKEEPER ROMANCES
Lawfully Held
A K-9 Lawkeeper Romance
Lawfully Defended
A S.W.A.T. Lawkeeper Romance
Lawfully Guarded
A Billionaire Bodyguard Lawkeeper Romance

HISTORICAL LAWKEEPER ROMANCES
Lawfully Taken
A Bounty Hunter Lawkeeper Romance
Lawfully Given
A Christmas Lawkeeper Romance
Lawfully Promised
A Texas Ranger Lawkeeper Romance
Lawfully Vindicated
A US Marshal Lawkeeper Romance

Blushing Brides Series:
The Billionaire's Reluctant Bride
The Bodyguard's Fake Bride
(Releases November 2019)

Standalone novellas:
Holly's Noel

LAWFULLY DEFENDED

Elle E. Kay

Faith Writes Publishing

266 Saint Gabriels Rd

Benton, PA 17814

ISBN: 978-1-950240-10-4

INTRODUCTION TO THE LAWKEEPER SERIES

There's just something fascinating about a man wearing an emblem of authority. The way the light gleams off that shiny star on his badge makes us stare with respect. Couple that with a uniform hugging his body in just the right way, confidence, and mission to save and protect, it's no wonder we want to know what lies underneath.

Yes, what echoes deep inside those beating hearts is inspiring. Certainly appealing. Definitely enticing. Although those ripped muscles and strong shoulders can make a woman's heart skip a beat--or two--it takes a strong, confident person to choose to love someone who risks it all every day. Anyone willing to become part of a lawkeeper's world might have a story of their own to tell.

The undeniable charisma lawmen possess make all of us pause and take note. It's probably why there are so many movies and TV shows themed around the justice system. We're enthralled by their ability to save babies, help strangers, and rescue damsels in distress. We're captivated by their ability to protect and save, defend the innocent, risk their lives, and face danger without hesitation. Of course, we expect our heroes to stay solid when we're in a mess. We count on them for safety, security, and peace of mind. From yesterday to today, that truth remains constant.

Their valor inspires us, their integrity comforts, and their courage melts our hearts--irresistibly. But there's far more to them than their courageous efforts. How do they deal with the difficulties they face? Can they balance work and life? And how do they find time for love outside their life of service?

We want to invite you on a journey--come with us as we explore the complex lives of the men and women who serve and protect us every day. Join us in a fast-paced world of adventure. Walk into our tight-knit world of close friendships, extended family, and danger--as our super heroes navigate the most treacherous path of all--the road to love.

The Lawkeepers. Historical and modern-day super heroes; men and women of bravery and valor, taking love and law seriously. A multi-author series, sure to lock up your attention and take your heart into custody.

Visit The Lawkeepers on Facebook:

www.facebook.com/groups/430422374043418/

Join our mailing list::

https://landing.mailerlite.com/webforms/landing/t1v0t1

The Lawkeepers is a multi-author series alternating between historical westerns and contemporary westerns featuring law enforcement heroes that span multiple agencies and generations. Join bestselling authors Jenna Brandt, Lorana Hoopes, Elle E. Kay, Patricia PacJac Caroll, Evangeline Kelly, Ginny Sterling, and more as they weave captivating, sweet, and inspirational stories of romance and suspense between the lawkeepers -- and the women who love them.

The Lawkeepers is a world like no other; a world where lawkeepers and heroes are honored with unforgettable stories, characters, and love.

** Note: Each book in The Lawkeepers series is a standalone book, and part of a mini-series of sorts, and you can read them in any order.

*This book is dedicated to my Lord and
Savior, Jesus Christ.*

CHAPTER 1

Sergeant Fitzpatrick stood in front of the candidates with his usual scowl in place. Marguerite tried to read her boss's expression, but knew it was pointless. This was the third time she'd attempted to make SWAT. The first time she'd scored a 97 on the range, the minimum to be a candidate. The second time she scored a 99. She'd outpaced the men when it came to rappelling and excelled at negotiating. Unfortunately, when it came time to drag a 200 lb. dummy across the desert, she'd failed. Twice. Today she had faced that challenge a third and final time. She hadn't wanted to get bulky, so she didn't lift much weight, but this year she'd trained harder than ever before. After hours of practice dragging weight across rocks, dirt, sand, and stream, she was sure that this time she'd passed the test. The real question was did she want it or was she simply proving to herself that she could keep up with the men? It didn't matter unless she secured her spot on SWAT. If she was selected, she wondered if the men would be willing to accept her on their team.

Despite being outdoors, the smell of sweat and dirt hung in the air. Fitz voice boomed loud and clear, calling names to step forward. As the front row was dismissed, she felt that familiar knot in her stomach from concern that she too might be sent home. Holding her breath, she counted in her head to slow her heart rate.

"The three of you who remain are now on SWAT. You will report for basic SWAT course at six o'clock Monday morning. If you're going to be late, don't bother showing up."

Marguerite released the breath she'd been holding. This was it. After years of hard work, she'd finally made SWAT.

Fitz continued "If you make it through training, you will report to SWAT leader, Seth Jacobs for duty. You're training agent will give you the details you'll need."

On her way to the parking lot, she pulled out her cell and dialed her pal, Brady. "I did it."

"Seriously? You made SWAT?"

She grinned. "I did."

"Hold on a sec." The line got quiet for a moment. Then she heard Brady's muffled words. "Justine, Mar made SWAT."

Marguerite couldn't stop grinning and Brady's excitement only increased her own.

Brady continued. "Justine wants to celebrate.

Meet us at the coffee house? Fifteen minutes?"

"I'll see you there." It felt good to have friends who wanted to share in her victory.

A throat clearing behind her got her attention. "I've got to go. I'll see you shortly," Marguerite said.

"Congratulations." Fitz held out his hand to shake hers.

"Thanks, boss."

"I wanted to touch base with you."

"Okay."

"Governor Campos is counting on you. You know I don't play politics, and I hate to mention it, but it was made clear to us that a woman needed to pass. And soon. Today is a day for the record books. You are the first woman to make the Arizona DPS SWAT team."

"Did I pass on my own skill? Or did they put me through despite my scores?"

"That's why I wanted to talk to you. You may hear talk that you didn't pass muster on your own, but it's not true. You and Bob Masters scored the same. José Ruiz was two points behind you."

"I would've passed without the Governor's influence?"

"Yes. You succeeded on your own. You've got this. Keep that in mind."

"Thanks, boss."

"I don't want to see you back in the squad room. You're going to have to work harder than the others to keep this assignment."

"I know, sir."

"I'm confident you'll do well." Fitz turned and walked back toward the station.

Black vultures circled overhead as Agent Diego Campos knelt beside the body of the young woman discovered an hour earlier by farm workers in the lettuce fields. From the level of decomposition, she'd been there for some time, but the smell of rotting flesh remained potent.

"There was another body dumped in Maricopa County earlier this week. I talked with the sheriff out there and we thought it was time to bring in the feds." Sheriff Lorenzo pulled his baseball hat down lower.

"We've got to catch this butcher." The rookie deputy standing beside the sheriff said, following his statement up with a string of expletives. A look from his boss quelled his tirade.

"I only hope we can be of help, Sheriff." The breeze picked up and tumbleweed rolled by. A flash of white paper caught Diego's eye. "What's that by the tumbleweed? You think you can catch up to that?" He directed his question to the deputy.

"Yes, sir. I'll check it out." The rookie ran off in the direction of the litter.

"The kid is Deputy Davis. Joined us last year. He's a hot head, but he's a decent cop. Just needs direction."

"I'm sure he's great." Diego stood. "Now back to the victim. Any missing persons reported in your county?"

"Not a single one matching her description." Sheriff Lorenzo leaned down to take another look at the body. He pointed toward the ragged duct tape binding the victim's arms behind her back. "I'm hoping you can help us catch the monster who did this."

Diego brushed dirt from his hands. "I'll do my best."

"I'm going to head inside and take the statements of the women who found her. Catch up with you later?"

"Sure." Diego shook hands with the sheriff. "I'll wait here until the medical examiner arrives."

"I appreciate that, Agent Campos."

"It's Diego."

"Thanks for coming, Diego. Please keep me in the loop."

Diego watched as Deputy Davis hurried to

catch up with his boss. He wondered what was holding up the medical examiner. Shielding his eyes with his right hand, he looked out over the dusty road that ran along the Colorado River. This part of Yuma was lush compared to most of Arizona, but the whole state was in need of a drenching rain.

A van turned onto the access road and Diego raised a hand indicating the driver should stop.

"You must be Dr. Walsh."

"I am." The tall blond inclined her head toward the young man towering over her. "This is my assistant, Jeremy Noble."

"Agent Diego Campos. Nice to meet you both." Diego walked the short distance back to the body. The victim had been dumped with no regard for the life that once was. She'd been bound with duct tape, there were obvious ligature marks around her neck, and the little clothing she wore was torn and filthy. "You can see why Sheriff Lorenzo thinks we have a problem."

"I certainly can. We had a similar scene a few days ago less than ten miles from here."

"I'll need to get more information from you about that case."

"I'll have Jeremy put together a file for you with copies of everything we have."

Diego watched as Dr. Walsh expertly examined

the body and then loaded it into the van.

Once the medical examiner left, he hopped into the Chevy Suburban he drove when he was on duty.

The medical examiner's assistant met Diego at the door when he arrived at her office. "Dr. Walsh is waiting for you." He held out a folder. "Here are the copies she asked me to make you."

"Thank you." Diego pushed open the door to the inner office.

"Nice to see you, Agent Campos."

"Good morning, Dr. Walsh." He approached her desk. "Any findings to report?"

"Yes, that's why I called you here. Have a seat." She indicated a chair opposite her desk.

He sank into an upholstered chair. "What do you have for me?"

"Take a look at the reports Jeremy copied for you. I'll wait until you're done."

Diego took several minutes to read through the reports before glancing back up at Dr. Walsh. "Neither of these victims have been identified. Is that unusual?"

"Not around here. This close to the border, it can be difficult to identify the victims who may not be here legally and don't have proper identification. Most of them aren't in our missing persons databases. Their loved ones know they came here for better lives. They expect them to be out there making their dreams come true. It may take months of silence before they're reported missing."

"So, we have two Hispanic women, beaten, raped, and strangled. Now the question is who are they and why?" He leaned back in the chair and met her gaze.

"I can't help you there, but I can tell you that both of the women suffered malnutrition. They also endured long-term physical abuse." She leaned forward over the desk.

"Long-term?" He lifted an eyebrow.

"The scarring indicates it was over years, not weeks or months."

"Years of abuse. Maybe the killer held the women for years before disposing of them. That's highly unusual."

"That would be one explanation for their condition." She tapped the folder on the edge of her desk.

"Thanks, Dr. Walsh." He stood and shook her hand.

"You're welcome to call me Harper." She smiled coyly and touched his arm.

Harper Walsh was a stunningly beautiful woman. He'd noticed her mild flirtation, and found her attractive, but wasn't sure about mixing his cases with his personal life. "I appreciate that, Harper. Let me know when the toxicology results are in."

"It'll be a few days." She stood. "I carefully removed the duct tape and put it in an evidence bag. We also found skin cells underneath their nails. Do you want everything sent to the FBI's lab?"

"Yes, please. I'll call and request they expedite the results. Doubt it'll do any good. We each think our cases are the biggest priority."

"I'm sure that's true. I collected DNA from both of the victims for identification purposes, but unless their DNA is in the system it's unlikely to be much help." Harper smiled. "Thanks for stopping by, Agent Campos."

"It's Diego."

As he made his way out of the building, he thought about the beautiful blond medical examiner, and wondered if he should pursue a relationship with her. He quickly dismissed the thought, but left open the possibility of revisiting the idea when the case was over if they both remained unattached.

Diego quickened his steps when he heard a loud thunder clap. The accompanying lightning danced across the evening sky. The skies opened up before he got the Suburban's door open. He threw the soggy folder on the passenger seat and climbed inside. There was nothing as intensely satisfying as a magnificent storm, but he preferred to watch them from inside his office, not up close and personal.

The past two months, had been grueling. Marguerite knew that SWAT wouldn't be easy, but she hadn't expected to be so worn out, so quickly. The intensive basic training course was complete, and she'd spent the past month completing her training with the team she'd been temporarily assigned to work with. She'd been pleasantly surprised that the men had treated her with respect. Many of them acted like older brothers. She only hoped that once she was assigned a permanent team they would behave with the same consideration.

Standing on her screen porch, she relished the sensation of the wind and rain on her skin. Storms made her feel alive. The open door leading back into her living room slammed shut. She tried to open it back up to go inside, but it wouldn't budge. She'd unlocked the deadbolt to come outside, but the handle was somehow locked. Strange, since she scarcely ever locked the handle. She exited the screen porch by the door into the yard in her bare feet and ran toward the front of the house, hoping she'd left the front door open, but she was sure she hadn't. Her doors were always secure.

When she reached the front of her house, she noticed that the lights were out too. Looking inside, she saw the television wasn't on. Her electricity must've gone out. The front door didn't budge. It was definitely locked. When she'd come home from work, she'd placed her keys and cell phone in a bowl beside her badge and gun. She banged her head against the door in frustration. There had to be a way back inside without having to ask to use her neighbor's phone. She could climb in her bedroom window. She'd thrown it open to let the fresh air in when she'd gotten changed from work. Soaking wet in her pajama shorts and top, she made her way toward the bedroom and pushed the screen up. After hauling herself inside, she closed the screen and sank to the carpeted floor, grateful to be back inside. That was a mistake she wouldn't repeat.

A noise from her walk-in closet made her jump, her gray tabby sidled up to her and rubbed along her legs. "I guess I'm scared of my own shadow, huh girl? The guys would get a good laugh at me now. Big bad SWAT girl afraid of a kitty cat." Marguerite stood. "Come on, Shadow, I need to get changed, but then I'll get you some dinner."

After putting some cat chow in a bowl for Shadow, she ate cold leftover macaroni and cheese and waited for the power to come back on. She'd planned to spend the night watching a movie on the Hallmark channel. Instead, she reached for her Kindle Paperwhite, it had a lighted background, so she could read in the dark. Propping herself up on some pillows, she got comfortable, ready to settle in for the night.

The buzzing of her work cell called her away from her novel before she finished the first chapter. A quick glance at the screen let her know she was needed for her first real SWAT call.

⁕⁕⁕

Diego stood at the conference table examining evidence with his partner, Tom Cortez. A television in the corner had the news on with no volume. Tom pointed up at it. "Did you see the news report of a woman making DPS SWAT?"

"I saw it." He sighed. "It wasn't a surprise. One of my mother's pet projects. The woman probably didn't qualify, but she earned her spot by being a woman."

"Tell me how you really feel?" Tom snickered.

"Let's get to work." Diego pulled an evidence bag with duct tape in it out of the pile.

They scrutinized the duct tape. "They managed to pull a partial print from this, but there was no match in IAFIS. The killer in all likelihood knew his prints weren't on file, so wasn't as careful as he should've been." Tom picked up another evidence bag. "What's this?"

"Let me see that." Diego took it from him. "I sent a deputy to chase a piece of paper, but I didn't see it again until now. I thought he'd either lost it or it was nothing."

"Looks like something to me."

"It sure does. I wonder why he didn't bring it to my attention at the scene."

"Maybe because he works for the sheriff, not you."

Inspecting the note, Diego felt a chill up his spine as he read the words on the crumpled paper. Five simple words. "Stop me if you can." Whether it was a taunt or a plea for help, it certainly shouldn't be ignored. "Did forensics get prints on the note?"

Tom looked through the reports. "I don't see anything."

"Let's get it back to them and make sure they didn't miss something."

"Sure thing." Tom turned to leave the room, but the buzzing of his phone stopped him. "DNA results are in. Two distinctive profiles: one from under the nails, the other from saliva on the duct tape."

"I guess the idiot ripped it with his teeth?" He inspected the duct tape. "It does kind of look like he may have. Did they run it through CODIS?"

"They ran it. No match on the duct tape, but we got a match on the DNA under the nails and an address to go with it. Carlos Valdez. On parole. Did time for robbery, assault and battery. Suspected gang affiliations."

"Praise Jesus. Looks like we have our man." He stuffed the evidence back into the box. "Let's roll out."

Ten minutes later, they were knocking on the door of Valdez's rental house. The windows were shuttered and there was a foul odor coming from the place. When nobody came to the door, they decided to stake out the house and wait on their warrant.

Sipping Mountain Dew that had long grown warm, Diego made a face. "Any progress on that warrant?"

"It's on the way."

"Thank goodness. I don't think I can sit here much longer."

When Agent Mertz arrived with the warrant, Diego and Tom approached the door to serve it. The younger agent stayed back. Tom kicked the door open when it remained unanswered. Inside they encountered a Hispanic man in his late twenties holding a knife to the throat of a young female. Diego kept his gun trained on the man, while he checked out the commotion in the adjoining room with his peripheral vision. There was another man holding a gun on a hostage. "Tom, let's go." He took a step back. "Don't hurt the hostages. We're leaving." The two of them slowly backed out of the house. What he expected to be a simple arrest had quickly turned into something else entirely. He shouted back to the rookie agent. "Get SWAT out here. Now."

***

The team assembled at headquarters. SWAT usually ran five man teams, but theirs was seven men. They were a man down when the three of them graduated. Once they'd gained some experience they would be dispersed to other teams. Marguerite hoped to secure the solo spot on this team. Loaded down with gear, they piled into the van. Adrenaline pumped through her veins. This was the moment they'd trained for. It was time to find out if she had what it took to do the job.

Their team leader, Seth Jacobs made eye contact with each of them in turn "Are we ready?" He waited until they nodded then got on with the briefing while the driver took them to the location. "We have a hostage situation. It was an attempt to serve an arrest warrant on a homicide suspect that went terribly wrong. There are hostages. Our snipers will set up on nearby rooftops. Here is the aerial view." He laid the page down in front of the snipers, Miguel and Jerry.

He laid down another page with a drawing of the house and pointed to a basement door. "I'm hoping we can breach here. The plan is to keep them distracted out front while we breach the back." He looked at the three newbies. "Remain with your assigned partner. You'll remember that we work in two man teams within the larger unit, so with two snipers and a negotiator, that leaves only two teams. Make sure you have your partner's back." She'd been assigned to work with the SWAT leader himself.

Bob Masters asked "If FBI is on scene why are we going in?"

"There are only three field agents on scene. Their nearest SWAT team is much farther away than we are."

"We're there to make the FBI look good?" Masters raised an eyebrow.

"We're going in to do our jobs. If you don't like that, you're welcome to step down from SWAT and go back to writing traffic tickets."

"I was kidding."

"I can appreciate a sense of humor, but save the kidding for the station, Masters. In the field I need you at your best." Jacobs lowered his face-shield over his eyes. The van came to a stop. "Roll out."

Marguerite stayed close to Jacobs as he

approached the FBI agent.

"Anything new, Agent Campos?" Jacobs asked.

"We need a clear shot. One of them has a knife to a woman's throat. Another has a gun on a hostage. We count at least four other hostages with him on the first floor, but there may be more in the basement. Thick concrete walls. We've got a thermal imaging drone on the way. It will give us a clearer picture." The agent ran his fingers through his thick dark hair.

"If we have the time," Jacobs said.

"Exactly. Is your team in place?"

"Yes. Kinicki and I will go in the front. The rest of my team is preparing to breach the back on your order."

"Perfect." He tossed his megaphone into his SUV. "Thanks for getting here so quickly."

"Doing our job."

"Did you bring a negotiator?"

"We're all trained negotiators, but I have my best man on it."

"Does he need the megaphone?"

"He has one."

"Let him know we're ready for him to do his thing."

Jacobs spoke a few words into his phone and Stevenson's voice filled the air.

CHAPTER 2

The men inside appeared to get more agitated with every word Stevenson spoke. Jacobs ordered him to halt the negotiations.

Marguerite watched as the drone was deployed. It flew close to the building and the suspect attempted to shoot it down through a first floor window. The agent manning the drone said, "We've got at least twenty warm bodies downstairs."

Miguel's voice came over the radio. "I have a shot. Should I take it?"

"Stand down. Let's see if we can take him alive. Keep your sights on him," Agent Campos said.

"We're going in. Kinicki stay close," Jacobs stood assault rifle in hand.

They approached the front door while the rest of the team approached the rear basement door. "Go." Jacobs spoke into the radio.

Tossing in a smoke bomb, Jacobs entered the

building. She followed close behind. A sound of someone running up the stairs drew their attention. They followed, clearing rooms along the way. Marguerite could hear the rest of the team down below. A split second after they entered the bedroom, the suspect tossed his weapon down, pushed the girl away from him, and put his hands up. "Down on the floor." The assailant complied with the order. She cuffed him while Jacobs covered her.

"Where are the other hostages?" she asked.

"Downstairs with Carlos."

"Does this Carlos have a last name?" Jacobs asked as she pulled the man to his feet.

"Valdez."

"And you are?"

"Alejandro."

"Last name?"

"Valdez. We're brothers."

Marguerite saw the figure approach from behind her boss, she raised her gun "put down your weapon." She fired as Jacobs spun to face the threat.

Jacobs bent down and checked the pulse. "Let's see if we're needed downstairs."

They arrived downstairs to find the rest of the team attempting to calm the hostages. Marguerite had never seen anything comparable, there had to be thirty women huddled in a fifteen by fifteen concrete room. Upon further inspection, she realized some of them were children, doubtless no more than fourteen or fifteen years old. The realization appalled her.

Putting on a mask of professionalism to hide her shock, she approached the youngest of the girls. "Estás seguro." She gently guided two girls toward the door. "You are safe." Once they were settled with the EMTs, she hurried back inside. Together the team and the agents hustled the rest of the women out of the cellar until they lined the sidewalk in front of the house where troopers and EMTs attended to them.

Jacobs stood beside her. "You did well today."

"Nothing about this day was good."

"It was a clean shot."

"I know."

"There may be trouble."

"I figured."

"Just remember, it was a proper shooting."

"I will."

"You still want to be part of SWAT?"

"From what I understand most of SWAT work ends peacefully without loss of life."

"It does."

"I'd like to stay, so I can see that happen."

"Glad to hear it. You'll make a fine addition to our team. I'm pulling for you."

Jacobs left to assemble the team to head back to headquarters. Marguerite found herself waiting by the van. She put her hands in her pockets, but the shaking wouldn't stop, so to distract herself, she took in her surroundings. There were DPS Troopers and FBI agents scattered about the scene. The troopers were mostly former colleagues. There was the agent who'd called them in on the case standing beside another man that appeared to be his counterpart. A short distance from them was a younger agent who appeared to be daydreaming. She thought it might be a coping mechanism. It must be difficult to face the situations they did each and every day. She certainly didn't want to relive this nightmarish SWAT call. Agent Campos strolled over to her. "Marguerite Kinicki, correct?"

"How do you know my full name, Agent Campos?"

"Call me Diego. Everyone in Arizona knows the name of the first female who made DPS Swat. When does the media tour start?"

"It doesn't." She tried to control the shaking in her hands. "What's going to happen to them now?" She waited for his answer.

"To the ladies? They'll be treated medically. We'll find out where they came from and try to reunite them with their families."

"Do you do that yourself?"

"No. That will be handled by another team. I'll interview them, of course. We need to find out exactly what was happening down there. Some of the story is obvious, but they'll have more details to share once they overcome their fear."

"Does that ever happen?"

"Not really. There is no recovering from what they endured."

"I didn't think so. What about the younger girls?"

"They may be more resilient than you'd expect."

"Looks like we're loading up."

He took a card from his wallet. "If you want to check up on the girls I can make it happen."

His hand brushed hers as she took the proffered card. The brief touch sent a jolt up her spine. In all probability it was from left over adrenaline following the shooting, at least that's what she told herself. "Thank you."

The team started loading into the van and she took her place between Bob and José. She listened intently as the others gave Jacobs a rundown of their involvement in the mission.

When he'd gotten the lowdown, he leaned forward. "Okay, listen up." Their eyes focused on him. He inclined his head toward Marguerite. "As you are all, no doubt, aware by now, newbie here shot and killed a suspect. He approached me from behind. Armed. It was a proper shooting. She's not to be bullied by the press nor by the DPS Investigators who will be conducting the inquiry. Am I clear?"

"Clear as mud."

"Excuse me, Masters?"

"Joking. Forgot to save it for the office, sir."

Marguerite fiddled with her watch. She knew Bob joked around when feeling pressure. His kidding didn't bother her, but she considered what might come to pass and whether or not she would be in for a difficult stretch. Her hands shook from taking the shot and she wondered how soon it would subside. Would the investigators think she'd been trigger happy because she'd shot several rounds? She'd reacted instinctively, but had followed protocol. Her gut churned at the thought of those women and girls huddled up in that cellar. She wasn't sorry she'd shot one of the men who'd kept them there. The only witness for her would be Seth Jacobs. Alejandro would surely claim she'd used unnecessary force to subdue his brother. Would she be treated fairly or would she be railroaded? She was fairly certain her shooting would be deemed good eventually, but what would she have to endure in the meantime?

The silence in the van was finally broken when one of her new teammates slapped her on the back. "Good job," he said. Grunts of approval from the rest of the team followed.

⁘

Marguerite picked up the telephone three times before she got the courage to dial. Diego answered on the first ring. "Well if it isn't super SWAT girl, Marguerite Kinicki."

"How do you know who it is?"

"I'm FBI, remember?"

"Caller ID?"

"Just like everyone else."

"My number is supposed to be blocked."

"Such is life."

"I was wondering if you were true to your word. May I see the girls?"

"Of course. I'm headed over there now. You want me to pick you up?"

"I can drive."

"I'd prefer to pick you up."

"Why?"

"Are you working today?"

"Barring an unforeseen emergency, no."

"Then after we visit the girls, I'll take you to dinner."

"Like a date?" There was no controlling the flutter in her chest at his suggestion.

"Yes, a date."

"Umm." Tongue-tied she couldn't find the words to answer him.

"It's not a requirement for seeing the girls."

"I didn't think it was."

"I'd like to take you out, but if you say no, we'll still visit the girls."

"I'd like that."

"Like what? To see the girls without the date or with the date?"

"I'd like to have dinner with you, I think."

"You only think?"

"I don't know you. So, yeah. I think."

He chuckled. ""I'll take it for now. Pick you up in thirty minutes."

"Don't you need my address?"

"I've got it."

"I don't think I want to ask how."

"Probably not."

Marguerite felt the heat envelop her as she

walked out her front door twenty-eight minutes later. She slid into the passenger seat of his pickup truck. "It's hot enough to fry bacon on the street."

"That it is, but I've got the air cranking, so it shouldn't be too uncomfortable."

"How far away are the ladies?" She fastened her seatbelt.

"Not terribly far. A little over an hour."

"Where are they being kept?"

"We have them at a makeshift safe house. It's a rundown abandoned motel. It's safer than having them at one of the local hospitals. I don't think the Valdez brothers were at the top of the food chain on this trafficking operation. We need to keep the ladies safely hidden away from whoever is running the show until we can send them home."

"I can't imagine what they must've gone through."

"You don't want to," he said.

"No. I don't."

"How do you know that once they go home, they won't be brought immediately back into this life?"

"We don't. I wish I could tell you that once a person is reunited with their loved ones everything goes well, but that isn't always the case."

"I figured that."

"There is a team of volunteers from Elena's House of Hope at the safe house. They work with us on cases like this, but they also have long-term programs for domestic victims to help them begin to recover and slowly acclimate into society. They're required to vet volunteers through us, so it's difficult for them to find enough help. If you're interested in hooking up with them, I can talk to Elena."

"Maybe. I'm pretty busy with work, but I might be able to volunteer some time."

"I'll introduce you to her."

"Will she be there?"

"Probably."

Diego put on the radio and she passed the time singing along to the country station, while he tapped out the drum beat on his steering wheel. "Where is this safe house?" She noticed they were driving away from town and into the barren desert.

"If I tell you that I'll have to kill you."

She laughed. "It can't be much farther."

"It can't?"

"No. If we go much farther, we'll be in California."

"You are correct. That's where we're going."

"Across state lines?"

"It's a perk of being a fed. I'm not bound by state lines." He glanced over at her. "We're nearly there. It's just across the border."

"And where did you intend to take me to dinner out here in the middle of nowhere?"

"If I told you that—"

"You'd have to kill me... yeah. I hear ya."

His low chuckle elicited butterflies.

"Can you turn that up?" she asked.

The voice on the radio said "confirmed shooting of an unarmed undocumented immigrant in the take down of an alleged stash house."

"They can't be talking about you. Carlos was armed and it wasn't a bust on a stash house."

"You missed the part where they mentioned the first female DPS SWAT Trooper."

"Oh." He squeezed her hand. "The press got it wrong. It'll get corrected."

"Too late. Once it's out there, it's out there."

He pulled into a spot. "Try to put it out of your mind for a while. I'm going to be interviewing the victims. You're welcome to accompany me as an observer or I can set you up with Elena."

"I think I'd prefer to go with Elena. The girls

might get defensive around a man.”

“You don’t think I’m charming enough to get through their defenses.” He gave her his best disarming smile.

“It won’t work on them.”

“That means it did work on you.”

“I plead the fifth.”

“It definitely worked on you.” He reached for her hand and brought it to his lips.

There was no controlling the involuntary shiver that followed.

⁂

Marguerite was taken aback by Elena’s beauty. She wondered why Diego would show interest in her with such a beautiful woman around. The two of them seemed to have an easy camaraderie.

“So, did you meet Diego at yesterday’s raid or did you already know each other?” Elena asked.

“We met yesterday.”

“You’re the SWAT Trooper they’re talking about on the news?”

“Yes.” She twirled her silver bracelet.

Elena tuned a television to a cable news station.

“This is unreal. He was armed and about to

shoot my SWAT leader in the back."

"It's the culture. Everyone is anti-cop these days. You almost come to expect the lies."

"I didn't expect this. Especially not on my first assignment with SWAT."

"Try not to let it get you down. Look." Elena pointed to the television. "They said our mother is coming up next."

"Your mother?"

"Diego didn't tell you?"

"Tell me what?"

"Governor Estelle Campos is our mother."

"Wait. You and Diego are brother and sister?"

"He didn't mention that either?"

"No. He didn't. I was wondering if you two were an item."

Elena bent over laughing. "I wouldn't date him if we weren't related. I know too much about him."

"I guess I should be careful."

"Definitely, he was a player once, but he's calmed down since he found Jesus." They watched as the governor was introduced. "My mother will defend you. Wait and see."

As Elena promised, Governor Campos came out in support of Marguerite. They showed a clip of the SWAT leader defending her, as well. It was humbling to see people she barely knew putting their own reputations on the line to defend hers.

"Are you still up for visiting with the girls?"

"I am." Marguerite stood up taller and pushed her emotions down. "This is something I need to do."

"Thanks for being here. It will mean a great deal to Isabella and Sofia. They're the youngest girls you helped to safety yesterday. They've been asking for their angel."

"Is that true?"

"I wouldn't have said it if it weren't."

She pushed open one door and then knocked gently on another door. "Isabella, Sofia? I brought your angel to see you."

The door opened and one of the girls threw her arms around Marguerite.

"That would be Isabella that nearly tackled you. Sofia is the shy one."

Marguerite hugged Isabella back and then reached out to Sofia who came slowly to join them. She put her arm around the girl's shoulder. It was clear she wasn't comfortable with touch, so she backed off. "I'm glad to see you both."

"You spoke Spanish," Sofia said.

"I did. I didn't know you could speak English."

"No good."

"Your English sounds good to me."

The girl smiled tentatively. "Going home to Madre."

"I'm pleased to hear that. Are you sisters?"

Sofia nodded.

"May I ask where you were taken from?"

"Columbia."

"Were you taught English there?"

"Some. Alejandro made us practice often. He tell us it's not good."

"He told you that your English wasn't good?"

"Sí."

"I understand you, so it must be good."

"Gracias."

The group moved to the kitchen and worked together to prepare a meal for the women. The girls didn't need to be asked, they voluntarily chopped vegetables, washed dishes, set tables, and did whatever else they could do to help.

"The girls are hard workers" Marguerite said.

"You'll find that to be a consistent trait if you choose to volunteer with us. It's the culture in South America. The girls are raised to be diligent and helpful. I'm not suggesting that we American women are lazy, but..."

Marguerite grinned. "Yes. I believe you may be saying exactly that, and I think it may be true after seeing these young ladies in action."

As the women began filing into the room and taking their places at the tables, Diego appeared in the doorway. Marguerite noticed several of the women visibly cringe at his presence. She wondered if it was simply because he was a man, or if it was because he'd questioned them.

"Ready?" he asked.

"I am." Turning to Elena she said, "Thank you for having me. I would like to volunteer. Can you send me the necessary paperwork?" She handed Elena a torn scrap of paper she'd written her email address on.

Elena's smile was genuine. "I will."

Diego pulled out the chair for Marguerite. As she scooted past him, he let himself breathe in the light floral scent she wore. He'd brought her to his favorite dining location. The food was consistently superb and the views over the golf course were magnificent. He wasn't sure why he'd asked her out. He'd nixed the idea of dating Harper because they were working a case together, yet Marguerite showed up in the middle of the same case and he couldn't stop himself from asking her out. It made no sense. Harper was just as beautiful, if not more so, but there was something about Marguerite that drew him in. It wasn't something concrete that he could name, but it was undeniably real.

"I hope you'll like this place as much as I do."

She grinned. "I'm sure it will be great."

Leaning in close to her, he pushed a piece of hair away from her eyes. "I'm definitely having steak. The chef knows how to cook it to perfection."

"Steak it is, then." She closed her menu.

"I'm glad to see you're a carnivore rather than a salad nibbler." Once they'd ordered, and the server brought their drinks, she made eye contact. "Why did you ask me to dinner?"

"I felt something between us yesterday that I wanted to further explore."

"Your mother didn't ask you to keep an eye on her latest project?"

"Elena told you who our mother is?"

She twirled her bracelet as she spoke. "She did."

"My mother is not the reason I asked you out."

"But you will report everything I say to her?"

"Not unless there is something you want her to know."

"Okay. Good. Then I'll try to relax." He could

see the distrust in her eyes. He wondered how she'd been burned in the past.

The food came and he took her hands in his before saying grace. It didn't surprise him that she seemed bothered by the prayer. He didn't want things to be awkward between them, but his faith came first. "I'm a Christian, Marguerite. Does that bother you?"

"Honestly, I'm not sure. I have a close friend who is a Christian and I'm growing fond of his wife, who is a woman of faith, but I don't like being preached at."

"I'll try not to preach at you, but may I ask you a question."

"I guess." She took a bite of her steak. "This is delicious."

"Yes, it is." He leaned forward. "Did you ever consider Christianity?"

"Sure. I attended church frequently as a child."

"Was your church about religion or Christianity?"

"What's the difference?"

"If you want to find out, I will happily show you." He leaned back in his chair.

"As long as it doesn't involve giving me a list of what not to do."

"You've got a deal."

They ate the rest of their meal in a comfortable silence. When they finished he drove her home.

After he pulled into her driveway, he took her hand in his. "I had a nice time tonight."

"Me too."

"May I see you again?" he asked.

"When?"

"How about tomorrow night?" He dropped her hand and brushed the hair from her face, so he could better see her eyes.

"Isn't that rushing things a tad?"

"I don't think so. No."

"Are you sure you want to be seen around town with me? My situation may get uglier before it gets better." She looked down at her hands.

"Then I'll stick around and help fight off the riffraff."

Her smile nearly undid him. He traced his knuckles along her jawline. "You are a beautiful woman, inside and out."

"You barely know me."

"You wear your heart where anyone looking can see it."

"I hope you're wrong." She spun her bracelet. He found her nervous habit cute. And telling.

"I'm not." His insides melted when she leaned

close. He knew she was anticipating a kiss, and he stared at her lips for a protracted moment noting their perfect shape. When she bit her bottom lip, desire nearly overwhelmed him. Then she turned away and let herself out of his truck, disappointment sat like a rock in his gut. He'd wanted to pull her into his arms, but his better judgment left him indecisive. He had to know she shared his faith before he let himself get too involved, but with her so near and her perfume intoxicating him, it would be easy to give in to temptation.

Before she closed the passenger door, he said, "I would've opened the door for you."

"I'm sure you would've. You're obviously a gentleman." She grinned. "To a fault."

"I'll pick you up at seven tomorrow night?"

He was relieved when she nodded. He watched as she let herself into her house. If he'd been inclined to join her inside, he had a feeling she would've welcomed him, but his self-control was under enough strain without adding to it.

CHAPTER 3

Marguerite hurried from headquarters to her sister's salon. She didn't want to miss her four o'clock appointment. The smell of acrylic nails assaulted her the moment she crossed the threshold. The bell over the door alerted the petite receptionist to her presence.

"Hi Lisa, I love the purple highlights."

"Thanks, Mar." The other woman, patted her hair. "I love them too. You're scheduled for a cut and style with Florence, followed by a manicure with Jane?" Lisa asked.

"Yeppers."

Flo will only be a few more minutes. Have a seat and she'll be with you shortly."

She took a seat and grabbed one of the magazines to thumb through. Soon, Florence came out and practically dragged her to her station. "I cannot believe you didn't call me."

"I guess you saw the news."

"You know I don't watch the news. Depressing stuff. Every client that comes in here is telling me how my sister shot an unarmed Mexican."

"It isn't true."

"Do you think I don't know that? Of course it's not true, but you should've called me anyway."

"Why?"

"So I could be there for you. That's why."

"I know you're there for me. I was out most of the day yesterday and then I had a date last night."

"A date?" Flo picked up a brush and ran it through Marguerite's long strands. "Tell me more."

"He's a gorgeous male specimen."

"Is he now? Details. Tall, short? Hair and eye color?"

"He's around six foot tall. He has dark wavy hair and eyes like a chocolate caramel latte."

"You're smitten already."

"Am not."

"A chocolate caramel latte? You don't talk like that. You're smitten." She put down the brush and picked up a comb and scissors. "What is he Italian? Mom and Dad would be pleased."

"No. He's not Italian. He's American same as me."

"It's okay to appreciate your heritage. It doesn't make you any less American." She trimmed as she talked.

"He's Hispanic. I don't know any more than that."

"You didn't ask him?"

"It didn't come up."

"Huh."

"He's Governor Campos' son."

"He's Guatemalan then. At least on his mother's side. We'll have to google his dad. You're dating the governor's son?"

"Hardly. We had one date."

"And are you planning to see him again?"

"Yes. Tonight."

"I've got news for you, girl. Two dates, two nights in a row." Flo pointed at Marguerite with the rattail comb. "You're officially dating the governors son whether you know it or not."

Two hours after she arrived at the salon, she left with perfect hair and nails. If she hurried she could still shower before Diego arrived to pick her up.

Diego looked up from an autopsy report as his partner continued his monologue on the benefits of the antioxidants in coffee. "Can we get back to the case, Tom?"

Tom smacked the steering wheel with his left hand. "You should drink coffee, Diego."

"It's not my thing. I prefer Mountain Dew."

"That stuff will rot your insides."

"Maybe so." Diego knocked Tom's hat off his head. "Now back to the case."

"The case doesn't make sense. If they were making money off the girls, why would they start killing them?"

"I don't think they did," Diego said.

"But the rescued women identified the photographs of the victims."

"Yes. They did."

"Carl Valdez' DNA was found under the second victim's fingernails. So he struggled with her, for sure. The cases are nearly identical, so they have to be the same assailant."

"I agree. Yet, I don't think Valdez is our guy.

"You can't have it both ways. He can't be the perp and not be the perp at the same time. His DNA was on the victim. He was at the house where they were holding the girls. What more do you need?"

"I have a theory, but I need more evidence."

"What's your theory?" Tom asked.

"I think he is both. I think he's guilty of plenty, but he's not the killer. What if they were selling off the 'old stock' as they bring in newly acquired girls?"

"You mean selling off the girls they no longer need to other traffickers?"

"Or selling them to whoever else wants them."

"It's an interesting theory. How do we test it?" Tom asked.

"We confiscated a laptop during the raid. Maybe it will have something useful."

"Do you have a computer forensics analyst working on it?"

"I gave it to Marcus, but I didn't give him any specific parameters. If I tell him what I'm looking for, he might find it faster. Let's stop by the field office."

"Sure thing." Tom directed the car toward the office.

Diego continued to go through his notes and the crime scene photos.

Tom pulled into their designated parking spot and they hustled inside. As they approached Marcus' office, the man stood. He pushed his glasses back on his nose with his forefinger. "I have something."

"What's that?" Tom asked.

"They've been running an auction on the dark

web."

"What kind of auction?" Diego asked, but he knew the answer before Marcus gave it.

"Women, girls, even a couple of boys." Marcus adjusted his glasses again. "It's sick. They got five thousand a piece for the women you found strangled. Why would somebody pay that much for a date and then kill her?"

"I don't think our guy is looking for a date. We need to stop him before he strikes again. If this site is shutdown, he'll go somewhere else." Diego clenched his teeth.

"That's the thing. It's not shut down. There is an auction going on presently. It has eight hours left." Marcus stretched. "There must've been more than one place where they were housing their victims."

"I knew those Valdez guys were low-level creeps. They weren't in charge of that operation. Take a twenty minute break, Marcus. I have a feeling we're in for a long night. I guess I'll be canceling my date."

Tom leaned back on Marcus' desk after the forensics expert hurried from the room. "You think there is a chance we'll find these kids?"

"We have to try."

"Maybe we should call in the BAU."

"Which unit? We've got crimes against

children, adults, and cyber-crime wrapped up in this mess."

"I'll call them. They can figure out which team to send, if any." Tom pushed himself away from the desk. "You call state and local. We've got to get a handle on this. We can get DPS out canvassing the street where the women were found. Maybe they'll find something we missed."

"There are no locals in that area." Diego pulled out his cell. "I've got a quick call to make then I'll call DPS."

Tom gave an exaggerated wink. "Give SWAT girl my love."

"She won't want it." Diego walked away.

<hr>

Marguerite was disappointed. She'd been excited for their date. It was foolish. She barely knew the guy. Yet, something about him made the butterflies in her stomach dance. She told herself it was indigestion. Why did she feel the need to romanticize her silly emotions? The jolt of electricity she'd felt when she'd touched him was real enough, but she'd had her share of romantic entanglements. They never ended well. And to get involved with an FBI Agent. That was crazy. Her job was insane enough, she didn't need to date someone with an equally outrageous work life.

It worked out okay for Brady, but Diego was no Justine. She smiled at the thought. No. He certainly wasn't. Diego was everything that attracted her in a man, and not only his looks, although they definitely didn't hurt. She forced herself to push aside thoughts of Diego.

Picking up her cell, she dialed Brady. It took three rings for him to answer. "What are you guys doing tonight? I'm not interrupting anything, am I?"

"Not at all. We're playing Scrabble."

"Do you two want to get out of the house? I'm dressed up with nowhere to go. My date canceled."

"Should I beat him up?" Brady joked.

"I don't think that would be the best idea. His reason was legitimate. Even noble. But, now I'm in need of friendly faces to cheer me up."

"We'll swing by and pick you up. How does Mia Roma sound?"

"No, thank you. Anything but Italian food, please. I've been eating my mother and sister's pasta creations for the past month. They colluded and spent a day cooking and freezing meals for me. Apparently, I'm incapable of taking care of myself since I'm not married yet. I didn't know unmarried women were unable to cook."

"In their defense, when was the last time you cooked for yourself?"

"It had been a few weeks, at least." She twirled the bracelet at her wrist. "It seems such a waste to cook for one."

"How about Chinese food?"

"Perfect."

"We'll pick you up in an hour. That will give princess special agent time to get ready." She could hear Justine shout 'I heard that' in the background.

Marguerite laughed. "I'm glad you stayed close."

"Me too." He cleared his throat. "Do you know which SWAT team you'll be permanently assigned to yet?"

"It's hard to say. I thought Seth Jacobs was going to offer me a permanent position, but after this publicity, he may decide to send me packing."

"He'd be a fool not to keep you on."

"Thanks for saying that. For now, I'm on administrative leave pending a full DPS investigation."

"Who didn't see that coming?"

"Exactly." She sighed. "If my body cam was functioning properly, and I believe it was, there shouldn't be a problem."

"We'll be praying."

"Thanks." Although she didn't pray herself, she appreciated how much prayer meant to Brady and Justine, so if they were praying, they believed it would help her.

<hr>

Diego stretched and worked the kinks out of his neck. It was past four o'clock, when he'd crashed on his office couch. A team of forensic analysts spent the night trying to trace the location the auction was streaming from, but the bouncing IP addresses made the task impossible. In the end, the auction had successfully completed, so their subsequent step was to try to discover where the transfer would take place. Glancing at his office clock he saw that it was nearly nine o'clock. He stood with the intention of going home for a quick shower and change of clothes.

The office door swung open and Dr. Walsh entered. Her waist-length blond hair was loose, not trapped in her customary bun. "I have something for you I didn't think could wait." She closed the door behind her.

"Thanks for coming, Harper." He met her in the middle of the office and shook her hand in a friendly greeting. "What is it you brought?"

"This is my autopsy report from the second victim, but there was something else."

His eyebrow shot up questioningly.

She bit her lip. "The second victim was pregnant. About two months along, I might've missed it if not for the lab work."

"Any chance of DNA from the fetus?"

"I dropped a sample off downstairs at the lab on my way up to see you."

"You're the best."

"I am, aren't I?" She stretched her long legs, which she showed off in a skirt that ended a few inches above her knees. "Here is the weird thing." She handed him a photograph, before leaning back in the chair and crossing her legs.

He looked at it for a picture for some time despite its repulsiveness. "They're being branded?"

"Yes. The question is by whom?" She stood. "Maybe talk to the women who were rescued see if they have similar marks."

"That should've been discovered in the medical exam and interviews, but I'll definitely revisit the safe house."

"I think that would be wise." Dr. Walsh strode to the door and with her hand on the door handle, turned back toward him. "Catch this scumbag."

"That's the plan, Dr. Walsh." He followed her to the door.

"I told you my first name is Harper. Use it."

"I will." He watched her sashay down the hall, then chastised himself for admiring the view. Any attraction he felt for Harper Walsh was purely physical. He forced himself to concentrate on the report she'd brought.

***

Marguerite had a towel wrapped around her wet hair when the knock on the door came. She peeked through the window and saw Diego standing in front of her door. She quickly tossed the towel onto a chair and ran her fingers through her mane. "Hi."

"Hi. I tried calling, but there was no answer."

"So, you dropped by?"

He grinned. "That's why I called, to ask if I could drop by."

"I must've been in the shower when you called." She held the door open. "Come on in."

He walked past her into the house and stood there fiddling with his keys.

"Want to sit down?" She led him out to her back screen porch, making sure the handle was unlocked this time.

They sat at a tiny bistro style table.

"I'm not sure why I'm here."

"You're not?"

"No. After missing our date last night, I felt like I had to see you."

"I was disappointed too."

"That helps." He chuckled. "I don't want to be the only one with feelings in the game."

"Do you think this is wise?"

"What's that?"

"You getting involved with me when I'm in the middle of a work crisis?"

"I'm not interested in you because of your job."

"What would your mother think?"

"I don't get dating advice from my mother." He took her hands in his. "You are beautiful without makeup, you know."

"You undoubtedly say that to all the women."

"There haven't been many women, but I digress." He stood and pulled her to her feet. He searched her eyes for permission before lowering his head to kiss her. Her telephone rang, interrupting the moment. Diego backed off while she answered it. He stood by the door awaiting her return. He'd nearly lost control when she'd wrapped her arms around his neck and her scent had surrounded him.

When she finally hung up the telephone. "Sorry, it was my sister. She has terrible timing."

"May I have another chance? Would you be willing to go to dinner with me now?"

"Now?"

"Yes."

"I'm not dressed for a date." She glanced down at her faded jeans and t-shirt.

"You're dressed perfectly for a casual date. How about burgers and ice cream?"

"Sure. Why not?"

Hurrying to ready herself, she applied lip gloss and mascara, pulled her hair into a ponytail, stuffed her 9 mm Sig in a holster inside her waistband, and grabbed her purse on the way back to the screen room where she'd left Diego waiting.

"I'm ready if you are."

He held the front door open. "After you, madam."

"Gracias, señor."

"Has anyone ever told you your Spanish is terrible?"

"Sí."

"I'm glad. I didn't want to be the first. I take it your family doesn't speak Italian?" He opened the truck door for her.

She waited until he climbed into the driver seat to speak. "My great-grandparents did, but they are long gone, my grandparents on both sides spoke a little, but my mother and father don't know any Italian."

He started the engine and pulled out of her driveway. "If you knew Italian, you would have no trouble with Spanish, they're very similar."

"I've heard that. I only learned Spanish to make life easier living in the southwest."

"I imagine it helps. At least you can understand people, even if you can't always make yourself understood, true?"

"Sometimes people speak too fast for me to pick it up, but I get most of it."

"I can help. I'll give you Spanish lessons."

"Why do I have a feeling I'll regret it if I say yes, but I'll regret it more if I say no?"

"You wouldn't want to say no because you would be turning down a chance to spend time with me." He wiggled his brows and grinned.

She laughed. "Can we have our ice cream first?"

"Not a chance. No dessert until you eat your burger." When he pulled into the ice cream shop he chuckled at the triumphant look on her face. "You may think you won, but they do sell burgers here. You will eat your burger before your sundae, young lady."

Sitting at an outdoor table was a win. Diego took a bite of his cone before tossing the rest to the birds.

"That's probably not healthy for them."

"Probably not, but look how happy it made them," he said.

"Me too."

"You too, what?"

"The ice cream made me happy." She giggled.

"Are you sure it isn't the company that made you happy?"

Ignoring the question, she pointed toward the back of the ice cream shop. "Look, I think it's a fawn."

"Odd place for a fawn."

The fawn took a few more steps into the parking lot. "Aw, he's so cute."

"How do you know it's a boy?"

"I don't, but I'm guessing. He's too precocious to be a girl."

"Ha! Yeah sure. Girls aren't precocious?" He smirked. "You should've seen my sister when she was younger."

"Here comes the momma deer." The doe

hustled the fawn out of sight.

"Are you ready to get out of here?"

"I guess." She stood. "You must have to work in the morning."

"I do, but I'm not ready for our night to end," he said.

"No?"

"No."

"Where to then?"

"You'll see."

"I'm game," she said.

"Excellent."

An hour later they were strolling along the riverbank.

"This is beautiful. I'm amazed you wanted to come so far on a work night."

"Any night can be a work night for me. I take advantage of the chance to live life as it comes. I could be bogged down in a case for weeks or even months with few breaks, so when I have a free moment, I live life to the fullest."

"Sounds logical."

"I'm not sure logical is the right word, but it works for me." He laced his fingers with hers. "How are you handling the investigation?"

"My SWAT leader, Seth Jacobs has my back.

He and the rest of the team are defending me with everything they've got. The union isn't hurting matters either."

"I'm glad to hear it. You deserve their support."

"The investigators said they spoke with you, as well."

"They did."

"Thanks for having my back."

"Not having been inside the building, I'm not sure I was much help. I tried to defend you by telling them what Jacobs said when you came out. He told me right away that you'd saved his life, so that's what I told them."

"The investigators act as if I had it out for the guy, like shooting someone gives me a thrill or something. It makes me wonder if they've ever had to pull the trigger on an actual person. Taking a life isn't something I take lightly."

"No. I would imagine not." He pulled her into his side and kissed the top of her head.

⁂

Diego drove along 110 listening to Tom's droning on about the myriad benefits of probiotics. One day it was antioxidants the following day he was talking about probiotics, he wondered which fad Tom would latch on to next. Hopefully it wouldn't be Yoga, he didn't want picture Tom doing downward facing dog or any other position. He caught himself chuckling and stopped.

"So, Tom, back to the case." He kept his eyes on the road.

"Do you think this lead will pan out?" Tom asked.

"I doubt it. I think they'll be gone by the time we get there."

"Then why are we going?"

Diego shrugged. "I don't know why we're going. Maybe because we have no quality leads."

"True enough." Tom stretched his legs. "Any news on the canvassing DPS was going to do?"

"Nothing concrete. They had a few neighbors mention seeing a white man at the house a number of times, but they got no decent descriptions of him. The girls claim not to have seen him. What about you? Find out anything new?" Diego opened the window to let in the fresh air.

"Nah. The note was a dud. No fingerprints or DNA. Not that DNA matters. We have DNA from multiple sources, and nobody to match it to. The notebook paper was commercially available, sold everywhere. No better luck with the ink. No fresh leads to go on."

"That's disappointing." Diego drummed his

fingers on the steering wheel.

"You still seeing SWAT girl?"

"How do you know I'm seeing Marguerite?"

"I'll take that as a yes."

"You didn't answer my question."

"It's all over the office. Everybody knows you're seeing her." Tom said.

"I'd love to know how that spread so quickly."

"I think it had something to do with the two of you being seen at a fancy golf course restaurant together."

Diego stopped drumming and his eyebrows shot up. "Who saw us?"

"I did." Tom smirked.

"You intentionally spread a rumor about me around the office?"

"It's not a rumor if it's true."

"I like her. Don't mess it up for me."

"How would I mess it up?"

"I don't know, but knowing you, you'll find a way."

Diego pulled into a secluded spot with some cover. "The transfer is supposed to take place over there, but in all likelihood it's a decoy location."

"No doubt." Tom pushed his seat back as far

as it would go and stretched his legs. "Might even be a set-up or an ambush."

"I doubt that. Why go to that much trouble? They're interested in making money not starting a war with the feds."

"Where are the state police?"

"DPS is here. They blend into the background well, don't they?" Diego said.

"They do." Tom peered into the distance trying to make them out.

"They even have a helicopter nearby."

"I hope we don't need it."

"I'll second that." Diego took out binoculars and searched the nearby hills.

A man dragging a woman from a van caught Diego's attention and he handed the binoculars to Tom. "Look, right there. It wasn't a set-up. Our techs are better than we thought."

"The title is analyst." Tom said.

"They're computer geniuses, does the term matter?"

"They are geniuses."

"SWAT is on standby." Diego quietly exited the SUV, Glock in hand. "I'm going to move silently through the brush and see if I can get a look at the buyer." He edged his way around the car and Tom got out and covered him. When he finally had a clear view of the exchange, a quick succession of shots took out the buyer and seller. Had DPS seen something he'd missed?

"Fitz, what was that about?" He spoke into his mouth piece.

"It wasn't us. Watch your six." A car was barreling toward him and Diego jumped out of the way with no time to spare. Tom wasn't as fast. "Get the EMTs over here now!" Tom's pulse was strong, but the force of the impact was brutal. His head gushed blood and his other injuries looked devastating. The head wound needed immediate attention, so he tore off his shirt and held it to the wound, praying for Tom to survive to go home to his wife and son. He felt responsible. He'd exited the car. He'd known something was off, but hadn't taken the time to warn his partner. His know-it-all partner annoyed him, but, nonetheless, he loved him like a brother. EMTs pushed Diego out of the way, quickly cleaned and wrapped Tom's head wound, then put him on a back board before transferring him to a gurney.

Diego watched the scene unfold as if in slow motion. Arizona DPS troopers and the other agents took chase after the vehicle that ran Tom down. Had the man in the car shot the suspects, if so, why hadn't he shot the agents? None of it made a lick of sense to Diego.

CHAPTER 4

Through much of the following hour, Diego sat at in the waiting room at the hospital while Tom underwent the first of several necessary surgeries, he took out his notebook and studied his notes. He tried to block out the antiseptic smell of the place, so he could concentrate on running through leads in his mind. Methodically he sorted through witness statements, autopsy reports, and every tiny bit of evidence trying to make connections where he could. He determined was that the killer was highly intelligent. He didn't make the buy himself, but had a middle man. Maybe more than one. He'd killed one of his middle men today when he realized law enforcement was on scene. He'd left no witnesses who could identify him. He was ruthless.

The auctioned girl survived her gunshot wound, she'd been hit with the same round that killed her captor. After a minor surgery, she'd been taken to recovery. He hoped to interview her the moment the medical staff allowed it.

A call came in while he sat there. There was a third victim. Somehow, he'd expected it. His gut had told him Valdez wasn't their killer. He was a creep and he wouldn't mourn for him, but he'd been a low level thug, not an intelligent psychopath.

Diego wasn't prepared to leave the hospital before Tom's family arrived, or before the surgeon gave him an update, so he asked another agent to meet with the sheriff at the scene, and promised to be there when he could get away.

When Tom's wife and son arrived, Diego told them what he knew. Together they waited for an update on Tom's condition. Slowly the time ticked by until finally the surgeon appeared and spoke quietly. "I can't make any promises, but he came through the first surgery and we're hopeful."

Diego promised Mrs. Collins that he'd be back to check on Tom as soon as he could and then headed off to the crime scene. Upon arrival he saw that Harper Walsh was already there. "Hello, Harper. Glad to see you're on the job."

"I've got your back, Diego." She looked over her shoulder at him and grinned. Her smile seemed out of place when he looked at the victim she knelt beside.

"Looks the same."

"It is the same." She turned the victim's ankle so he could see the brand. "Did you ask the victims from the raid if they had been branded?"

"Yes. I did." He balled up a fist in frustration. He wanted to hit someone. Preferably the man who'd done this. Likely the same guy who'd put his partner in the hospital. "They hadn't been branded and the thought that the other girls were terrified them. He has to be branding them after he purchases them from the auction."

"The wounds from the brand are well healed, so he holds them for a great deal of time before disposing of them."

"We've got to catch this guy."

"Yes. You do. I don't want any more Jane Doe's on my table." Harper and her assistant loaded the body into the van. "I'll call you when I have more. Any news from DNA?"

"Yes. They got a match on the duct tape and they're seeing if the profile could be the father of the fetus. It's not much without a match in CODIS."

"We'll talk soon." She got in the van and drove off with the body.

While he was interviewing the witnesses who'd discovered the body on their ranch, the press showed up in full-force. One particularly obnoxious journalist kept shouting questions.

When He finally gave in and talked to him, the reporter gave him a note. "I'm Jason Blake with nightly news. Can you confirm if this note is indeed from the serial killer?"

Diego inspected it. "Where did you get this?"

"It was delivered to the newsroom. Is it him? Can you tell us more? Do we have a serial killer leaving bodies in Yuma and Maricopa counties?"

"No comment. How many people handled this?"

The man took a lengthy drag on his cigarette. "Only me. I opened it myself."

"We'll need to get elimination prints from you."

"Sure. Whatever you need." The man crushed his cigarette under the heel of his shoe.

Blake walked away and Diego retrieved the cigarette butt and put it in an evidence bag.

⸻

Diego sat at Tom's bedside. The incessant beeping of hospital equipment was driving him batty. He'd had the nurse in several times to fix the IV, so it would stop beeping.

A few hours earlier, he'd sent Kara home to get some rest. She'd been at his side for more than forty-eight hours. He wondered if Tom could hear his voice. In case he could, he spoke aloud. "What are you doing, Tom? Your wife and son need you. If you don't want to keep going for yourself, at least do it for them. Besides, I didn't tell you about my last date with Marguerite. It was better than I could've dreamed. She's a special woman. I think she may be the one.

"Only if she comes to know Jesus, of course, but I'm hoping her reluctance is due more to not knowing the gospel than it is to rejecting it. Why am I talking to you about this? You're not a Christian. Which is another reason you need to pull through. If you want to spend eternity in the presence of the Lord you need to accept Christ as your Savior. Did you know that he died for your sins? Why haven't I talked to you about my faith? If you don't come back, I'm going to spend the rest of my days feeling guilty about not sharing the gospel message with you, so get better already, would you?"

The nurse came in for rounds and Diego fell silent. When she left, he opened his Bible and read out loud thinking maybe some of it would get through to Tom's consciousness. By the time, Kara returned a few hours later, he'd fallen asleep in the chair.

"Hey, Diego." She touched his shoulder.

He jumped. "Kara. You're back. What time is it?"

"A little after ten. Thought you might want to go home and get some rest before work tomorrow."

"I probably should."

He gave her a pat on the shoulder and made his way toward the parking lot. Before he got to his car, his phone buzzed. "Agent Campos speaking."

"It's Kara Cortez."

"Is everything okay, Kara?"

"Tom woke up. He's asking for you."

"I'll be right up."

The elevator seemed determined to move slower than ever before as he made his way back to Tom's room. The joy on Kara's face was a sight to behold. He stood in the doorway and allowed her another moment with the spouse she'd come so close to losing. When Tom looked up and saw him, he stepped inside. "It's about time you wake up. What are you doing sleeping the days away like some kind of sloth?"

"Glad to see you too, Campos."

"You asked for me?"

"I did. I was wondering if you caught the guy that ran me down."

"Not yet, DPS chased the car, but they lost it. We'll get him. Agent Mertz volunteered to help me out until you're back at work."

"Good. He's been helping out since the start, so you won't need to bring him up to speed."

"I'd rather you were there, but you need to rest, so you can fully recover."

"How's the girl?"

"She was shot, but she's expected to be okay."

"Thank goodness."

"No. Thank God."

"Yeah. That's what I meant."

"I'll let you spend some time with your wife. You'll see my ugly mug in here tomorrow after work."

"I'm hoping to be home by then."

"Don't count on it."

<hr>

Marguerite closed her vents, so the cold air would stop blasting her. Turning in the passenger seat to face Diego, she asked, "Are we lost?"

"Of course I'm not lost."

"Is that the typical man answer of I can't be lost because I'm a man and men don't get lost?"

"No. It's the truth. We're not lost."

"Where are we going? If you tell me where we're going, I might be able to tell you if we're going the right way."

"Marguerite, darling, I adore you, but please

stop with the lost talk."

"Fine." She turned back around in her seat and faced forward.

"Don't get mad." He glanced over at her.

"I'm not mad."

"Yes. You are."

"I'm not," she said.

"I thought we'd have a day of exploration. We're going to visit Salvation Mountain and Slab City."

"My sister visited there. She thought it was amazing. She's a Christian, so I'm sure it's different for her than it would be for me."

"You might surprise yourself and have a pleasant time."

"If I'm stuck with you, how can I possibly have fun?"

"You're a hoot and a half, girl."

"Seriously though, I'm sure you could make scouring a dump site delightful."

"What are you buttering me up for?"

"Nothing in particular. Simply accumulating brownie points for when I need them."

He took her hand and squeezed it. "We're nearly there."

"Thanks for this." She squeezed his hand back. "I'm nervous about the meeting tomorrow. I appreciate you trying to take my mind off it."

"You'll be cleared."

"I know." She stared out her window as the desert flew by. "It's a bit overwhelming though. It was my first fatal shooting."

When they arrived a few minutes later, he parked the truck, but made no effort to turn off the engine or get out. Instead he pulled her closer to him. "I didn't know it was your first shooting. Have you talked about it?"

"To the investigators, yes, plenty."

"To anybody else?"

"They made me see the department shrink."

"Mar, taking a life is always hard, but you made the only decision you could've at the time. You were choosing between the life of a man who has devoted his life to helping people or the man who was determined to murder him."

"Well, when you put it like that, it seems easy to reconcile, but he was a brother, a son, possibly even a father."

"He was a brutal thug, concentrate on the reality of the situation. You didn't have a better choice in that moment."

"I guess not." Reaching over, she took his hand.

He scooted toward the middle of the bench seat and pulled her into the circle of his arms. She inhaled the spicy scent of his cologne and snaked her arms around his neck. When he abruptly released her, she was taken aback for a moment, but then she noticed the car that had pulled up beside them. The driver and passenger were both staring.

"Are you ready to get out of the truck?" she asked. He nodded and started around to open her door, but she beat him to it. Taking his hand, she walked with him, settling for the nearly platonic contact.

The magnitude of the place astonished her. She'd seen pictures of Salvation Mountain, but they hadn't done the place justice. The artwork was enchanting and held her interest. Unfortunately, after about an hour of exploring, the lack of bathroom facilities had her begging to leave.

When they got back in the truck, Diego asked, "What did you think?"

"I'm not sure what to think." She crossed her legs and hoped they'd get to a restroom soon. "It was definitely interesting. I usually prefer the beauty of nature, but it had a special kind of charm. I enjoyed myself." She squeezed his hand. "I was especially fond of the company."

<hr>

Marguerite looked at the clock for the third

time. It was four-thirty, but she wasn't likely to fall back to sleep, so she might as well get out of bed. After stretching out the kinks, she threw off the covers. Once she was showered and dressed, she glanced down at her watch. Ten of five. Time was crawling by. It was going to be an endless morning. She made a cup of coffee with her Keurig and inhaled the scent of the strong brew. Flipping on the television, she sat down to watch the morning news. Afterward, it was still only five-thirty, so she made herself a smoothie which she poured in a to-go cup. She chose to head in to work early. The time wasn't going to move any faster at home, so she might as well jump back into the fray.

Headquarters was quiet when she arrived. Sitting down at her desk, she powered on her computer. It didn't take much time to go through department emails. She was leaning back in her chair drinking a cup of bad coffee when Seth Jacobs arrived with Sergeant Fitzpatrick on his heels.

"Good morning," she said.

"How's it going, Marguerite? You're early. Why don't you join us?" Fitz said.

She stood and followed them into the office. Fitz remained standing, and Seth took a seat. A moment later, at a knock on the office door, Fitz opened it and let Governor Campos into the room.

"Hello everyone. Glad to see everyone is here."

"Welcome, Governor." Fitz took his seat. "Why don't you have a seat?" He indicated an empty chair.

"That would be delightful. Thank you," Governor Campos said.

"The floor is yours," Fitz said to the governor.

"Marguerite, I came to congratulate you on your reinstatement. Your body cam footage has shown that the shooting was indeed justified."

"We knew it would." Jacobs stood to go.

"Yes, I've read your statement about the incident," Governor Campos said.

"Congratulations, Marguerite. You've also been requested for permanent assignment with Seth Jacobs' team. Assuming your acceptance of his offer, you will start today." Fitz stood.

"Thank you, sir." She stood and shook Fitz' hand. She followed him toward the door, but turned when she felt Governor Campos' hand on her shoulder.

"Would you talk with me a moment?" Governor Campos' coffee colored eyes held hers.

"Sure."

The governor closed the door. "I'm glad you didn't disappoint me. Your position in SWAT is important to the women's movement."

"I didn't sign-up to make a political statement."

"Nevertheless, you've done so, be it an unintended consequence or not."

"How so?" Marguerite spun her watch around on her wrist.

The governor laughed, but there was no mirth in it. "A woman on SWAT is a political statement whether you wish it to be so or not, but that isn't what I wish to talk to you about."

The churning in her stomach grew more pronounced. "Oh?"

"I understand you're dating my son."

"He didn't mention that he'd shared that with you."

"He hasn't." The governor pinned her with an intense stare. "I hear things."

"Yes, we've been out a few times."

"Excellent. It will do your career wonders to be seen with him. He's a respected agent as well as my son. Don't mess it up. The women's movement needs you to succeed."

"Am I understanding you correctly? You want your son to date me to help the women's movement?"

"Everything you do will be scrutinized by the press. Your taste in men matters."

"That sounds rather sexist. Governor Campos,

it was lovely to meet you. I'll perform my best at my job, but I'm not willing to be the women's movement poster child or to let my love life be decided by politics." She stood. "I like Diego. He's handsome and kind. I believe we could have a future, but I wouldn't date anyone for political gain."

Diego had made plans to take Marguerite out to lunch. He'd hoped she would be cleared and they'd have a reason to celebrate. When he took one look at her, he sighed. "What did she do?"

Marguerite sent daggers his way. "I assume you're referring to your beloved mother? Our esteemed governor?"

"I am."

"Did she suggest you take me out? Am I her project in more way than one?"

He put both hands on her shoulders. "No." He squeezed her shoulder and then tipped her chin up so she was looking in his eyes. "I am my own man. We went on the first date because I was attracted to you physically. We continued dating because I was attracted to you in every other way. I enjoy being around you."

"I want to believe you."

"Then why don't you?"

"Your mother. She left me feeling like nothing more than a political pawn."

"She means well."

"Are you sure?"

"Positive." He laughed. "Want to be let in on a little secret?"

"What's that?"

"I didn't vote for my mom. I don't share her political opinions." He pulled into a parking spot and hurried around to open the passenger door.

Marguerite got out of the SUV, but leaned against it. "She practically has you set to follow in her footsteps."

"That's her dream. It's not mine. I have no intentions of becoming a clone of my mother."

She breathed a sigh of relief. "I'm glad because I like you."

"You do, huh?" He leaned in close and brought his lips down to within inches of hers.

"Yes, I do."

"Good because I like you too." He whispered against her mouth. Lowering his lips to hers he kissed her gently, enjoying the taste of her flavored lip gloss. "I thought only teenagers wore flavored lip gloss."

"I like to do the unexpected." She deepened the kiss and he offered no resistance.

By the time he gained his senses and ended the kiss, several minutes had passed and the kiss had grown in urgency, as well as promise. She melted against him and he groaned.

"Let's go inside."

"Why do you do that?" Marguerite demanded.

"Do what?"

"Draw back? It took you forever to kiss me and now you're backing off."

"You know I'm a Christian. I take my faith seriously and part of that means I don't sleep around."

"Seriously? You're celibate?"

"More like I'm waiting for marriage this time."

"So, you haven't always been this way."

"No. Unfortunately, I haven't."

"Too bad I didn't meet you sooner."

He chuckled and took her hand. "How about a nice meal?"

"I suppose it'll have to do if that's what you want."

"It is." He laced his fingers with hers and pulled her along behind him.

***

Diego pulled into the parking lot at the Vulture

Mountains Recreation Area and found a spot. "I think we could both use some time outdoors."

"What a splendid idea, babe."

"I'm not sure that term of endearment suits me."

"I think it's perfect."

"Maybe we should work on your Spanish lessons, then you could call me something more suitable."

"Nah. I think I'll stick to 'babe'."

"I'm not going to win this one, huh?"

"Nope." She reached for his hand when he came around and opened her door. "How is Tom doing?"

"As well as can be expected. They sent him home yesterday."

"I bet he's itching to get back to work."

"He is. Let's hope they bring him back soon before he reads too many of those men's health magazines. He comes up with some crazy ideas from the articles in them."

"He's probably correct about most of it."

"Even if he is, I'm not changing my lifestyle to fit the most recent health fads."

"Me neither," she said. "How do you like your temporary partner?"

"He's okay, I guess. Talks too much and thinks way too highly of himself, but I can tolerate him. He works hard."

"That's good, I guess."

"Let's not talk about work anymore."

"Agreed. It's gorgeous here." She twirled around in a circle, grinning.

"Feeling a little silly, my treasure?"

"Yes. That's one of the things I adore about you, babe. I feel free to be myself, even when I'm at my goofiest."

"I'm glad. I wouldn't want you to be anybody else." He caught her mid spin and pulled her into his arms. "You're flawless the way you are."

⁕

Diego stuffed his keys into his pocket before opening the passenger door for Marguerite. "You ready for this?"

"I suppose." She stepped down from his pickup truck and her heel sunk into the soft ground.

"I should've recommended boots," he said.

"That would've been helpful."

"Elena said to meet her and Chaz by the ice cream concession stand."

"Sounds like a plan." Marguerite steadied herself by hanging onto his arm.

Forty-five minutes later, sitting on the bleachers, Diego looked down at the beautiful woman by his side. She'd obviously never been to a rodeo before, but she hooped and hollered with the crowd excited to see Elena's fiancé compete in the bareback competition.

Marguerite glanced at Elena, her hand fluttering over her heart. "I don't know how you can take the stress." Reaching over, she squeezed his thigh and the jolt of desire that shot through him made it impossible to concentrate on the show. "I would lose it if Diego was the one up there."

They watched with horror as Chaz was thrown from the bucking horse. The horse seemed suspended in mid-air over his body until it twisted at the last second and came down beside him. Chaz jumped to his feet and climbed the rail.

Elena smiled with relief. "Believe me when I tell you, I don't like him competing, but it's who he is, and I wouldn't want to change him. He's nearly perfect."

"I don't know if I could have that attitude." Marguerite's hand rested on his thigh again and he placed his hand over hers. Was she trying to send him over the edge?

Diego stood in order to break the physical connection without hurting her feelings. "I'm going to go grab us some hotdogs."

"Bull riding is coming up next, we'll hang out and watch while you grab the food," Elena said.

When Diego got back with the hotdogs he was heartened to see Elena and Marguerite were huddled together chatting like old friends. He sat beside them and passed out the food and drinks, before stuffing down two hotdogs, nachos, and a huge soda. It was nice to see Marguerite enjoying herself. He didn't love the rodeo, but he attended to support his best friend and his sister, so as long as it didn't conflict with work he tried to be at the local events where Chaz competed.

Walking back to the truck, Marguerite put her arm around his waist. He enjoyed the contact, but wanted more and knew she did too. He wondered how much longer he would be able to put the physical aspect of their relationship on hold without driving her away.

In the truck, she sat in the middle and played with his hair while he drove. This woman would be the death of him. He pulled into her driveway and walked her to the door.

"Are you going to come inside?" she asked in a sultry tone.

"You're killing me."

"That's kind of the goal."

He groaned and gave into the desire to kiss her, but soon she was opening the door and pulling him inside with her. Their kisses were urgent and passionate. If he didn't stop now, he wasn't going. She pressed closer to him and trailed kisses down his neck. It took every ounce of control he could muster to stop her. "I can't do this."

"Of course not." Her tone was chilly. "Why don't you have a seat? I'll get you a glass of ice tea?"

"That sounds great." He wasn't sure what he could say that would help her understand his dilemma. So, he sipped the iced tea she brought him, before leaving with one last chaste kiss. The taste of her raspberry lip gloss stayed with him the entire drive home.

Marguerite had a white knuckle grip on the steering wheel. She wasn't afraid of heights, but she didn't love them either. What had she been thinking letting Brady talk her into this?

"Where are we going?" Diego asked.

"To do something fun and adventurous with my friends."

"That's what I'm afraid of." He grinned. "It's revenge for the rodeo date, isn't it?"

She laughed. "Maybe a little."

When she pulled into the parking lot, Diego had the nerve to look excited. "Really? Hot air balloons. I've always wanted to try that."

"Then it's your lucky day. Brady convinced his wife Justine and me to do this and now I'm dragging you along."

"This will be fun." He brushed his lips across hers. "Wait and see."

"It better be or I'm going to murder Brady."

"Might not want to make threats in front of the FBI agent."

"I'll murder you afterward."

He held up his hands in mock surrender. "I'll behave."

Brady came out of the building and shouted for them to join him. Twenty minutes later the crew worked to inflate the balloon. The knots in her stomach grew tighter at the anticipation of being so far above the earth.

Putting his arm around her shoulders, Brady whispered, "You'll enjoy yourself once you're in the air."

"I guess we'll soon find out."

"If nothing else, you'll enjoy the time with Diego."

"What do you know about it?" she asked.

"I can see the way you look at him." He grinned. "You're a goner."

"You're a goner if I hate this."

"Justine will protect me."

"Sure she will." Marguerite put her arm around Justine's waist. "Girls stick together, so you might be out of luck."

Diego moved in closer to her and she released Justine to lean in to his side. Brady and Justine climbed into the balloon after their pilot, and then Diego assisted her. Once everyone was in the balloon, they soared upward. Diego sensing her nervousness, held her close to his body. After several minutes, she began to relax a little. The air was crisp and clean, so she breathed it in and let it steady her. Soon the spectacular views over the Sonoran Desert distracted her from stressing and she enjoyed herself. Diego didn't release her, even once they'd been in the air for quite some time. She wondered if her anxiety gave him the excuse he needed to be able to embrace her without the guilt that normally plagued him. He wouldn't hear any complaining from her. She let herself relax against him and enjoy the feel of his muscular arms around her.

The landing didn't go as smoothly as they'd hoped and the pilot put them in a mesquite tree a few feet from the road. The basket tipped over sideways. "I'm going to need each of you to carefully climb out, one at a time," the pilot helped Justine first, followed by Brady, her and Diego got out last.

"Did you see the look on Marguerite's face when we hit the tree?" Brady asked.

"I did." Diego answered. "She looked like she'd seen a ghost."

"You couldn't even see my face. You were behind me."

"I could." Justine answered.

Brady guffawed. Diego joined him in laughter. Soon they were cracking up over Marguerite's overreaction to their less than stellar landing.

The four of them met at the local diner for a quick bite to eat before going home. When they were back in her car on the way to her house where Diego had left his truck, she asked, "What do you think of my friends?"

"Brady and Justine are great. I'm puzzled as to how I haven't met her before being that we're in the same line of work. We often have need for explosive experts."

"She was in Virginia until recently when she and Brady got married."

"That would explain it. I'm sure I'll be seeing her on the job now that she's out here."

"I don't think she spends as much time on the job now that she's a boss."

"Must be nice."

"I'm sure. I doubt I'll ever find out."

"Why is that?"

"Being a woman in a man's job is hard enough.

I'm not sure there is any chance of rising through the ranks any more than I already have."

"What made you become a trooper?"

She pulled into her driveway and turned off the engine. "That's a tough question. My father was a trooper. He didn't think women belonged on the job. It frustrated him that testing was altered to allow women into what he thought were men's jobs. He thought that if they couldn't pass the same test as the men, they were putting their fellow officers in danger."

"What did you think of his opinions?"

"I agreed with him about the testing." She grinned. "I disagreed with him that a woman couldn't do the job. I set out to prove him wrong."

"Was he proud of you?"

"He was. I was able to pass the testing without any modifications. I showed him that it could be done."

"Where is your father now?"

"He was run down on the highway while writing a traffic ticket."

"I'm sorry."

"He was about to retire."

"Wow. Life is so unfair."

"My mother deserved to have that time with him, but he was snatched away."

She got out of the car and he walked her to the door. "You should let me open your car door, it makes me feel good."

"I'll try to remember in the future." She stood on her tiptoes and brushed her lips across his. He pulled her closer and took his time kissing her. "Are you coming in tonight?"

"It's probably best if I don't, mi tesoro."

"If you say so."

"Goodnight, my treasure." He smiled. "It loses something in translation, don't you think?"

"No. I love it in both languages. Goodnight, Diego." Inside the house, she let out a groan of frustration.

Marguerite didn't understand men. Most seemed to want nothing but sex. Diego wanted everything except sex. If his physical reactions were anything to judge by, he seemed to be attracted to her, but she wasn't sure how long she could stand his saintly attitude.

She picked up her cell and called Brady's house. "Hello," he answered.

"Brady, is Justine around?"

"She is, but she's getting ready to jump in the shower."

"Will you ask her if I can stop by? I need to talk to her."

"I'm sure she'll be okay with that, but hold a sec and I'll ask." The phone was silent for a minute before he spoke again. "She said she'd love it if you stopped by. She's tired of looking at me."

"Justine did not say she was tired of looking at you."

"Well, not exactly."

"I'll see you shortly." She disconnected the call and grabbed her purse from the hook in her bedroom closet.

Twenty minutes later, she was savoring the sweet and sour taste of a glass of lemonade on Brady and Justine's back deck. "Thanks for the lemonade. It's delicious." Their two German shepherds sat nearby. "I love the view from your deck."

"It is beautiful, isn't it?"

"Sure is."

"You didn't stop by to talk about lemonade and views, so what's on your mind, Mar?"

"You're a Christian, so I thought you might be able to help me out with some questions."

"What do you want to know?"

"As you know, I've been dating Diego for a while. He's a Christian and I get this feeling deep in my gut that he's going to dump me. He hardly touches me and when I try to make an advance on him, he pushes me away. I'm starting to feel unwanted."

"He's presumably trying to live his faith."

"That's what he said."

"It doesn't mean he doesn't want to be with you."

"It doesn't?" Marguerite spun her silver bracelet around her wrist repeatedly. "It sure feels like it does."

Justine placed her hand on top of Marguerite's to still them. "You will run into a problem if you continue dating and he truly desires to live according to his faith."

"How so?"

"Christians are not supposed to be unequally yoked. It means we aren't to enter into a relationship with a non-Christian once we've accepted Christ."

"So, he is going to break up with me?"

"Eventually, yes. He probably will. Otherwise, he would know that difficulties will arise."

"He's tried to talk to me about Christ a few times, but I've blown him off. He took me to Salvation Mountain and showed me a bunch of Bible verses. He explained what his salvation meant to him and how important Jesus was to him." She sighed. "I want to understand. I really do, but I don't get it."

"If you're not ready to accept Christ's gift, no amount of talking is going to help. You have to search for the truth on your own, asking the questions you need answered along the way. Once you do that, God will lead you to the truth."

"Search for the truth. It sounds so lofty and high."

"It may sound that way, but there is nothing greater than Christ's love and I do pray you come to accept His gift."

"But, if I don't, I can say goodbye to Diego."

"Honestly, you would be better off ending the relationship now then getting closer to him only to have him break your heart later."

"You think so?"

"I do." Justine closed her eyes as if in prayer. "Marguerite, I want nothing more than to see you come to Christ, but it's something you have to do for yourself not for a man. I'm afraid if I share the gospel message with you at this moment, you'll claim to accept Christ for the wrong reasons and if you don't believe in your heart, you won't truly be saved. Your eternal salvation is so much more important than any relationship here on this earth."

"What should I do?" Marguerite wiped away a tear. "I want the kind of romance that you and Brady have, and I thought Diego could be the one, but now I'm once again in a relationship that's falling apart."

"Brady and I both put Christ first and it makes it easier to please each other since we're both trying to please God. Until you accept Christ for yourself, a Christ-centered relationship isn't possible. My advice would be to let the man go. Then, take some time to search your heart and the scriptures. Who knows? Maybe later, you'll have come to Christ and you and Diego can try again."

"He'll be married and gone by then."

"If it's God's will for you two to be together, it will work out in the end. It will. But it is never God's will for us to purposely disobey His word. Many a marriage ended in divorce because a Christian intentionally married a non-Christian."

"My heart hurts."

"Are you in love with him?"

"I'm heading in that direction."

"Guard your heart until you're ready to give it to Jesus. He'll treat it better than any man can."

⸻

Marguerite had every intention of ending her relationship with Diego when she left Justine and Brady's house. It wasn't fair. Why did God put these crazy rules on His children? Justine seemed pretty sure that it couldn't work out and for some reason, Marguerite believed her. Something told her that everything Justine said was true.

Watching Brady and Justine's faith showed her that there was more to their Christianity than pretty words and she wanted what they had. She honestly did. If only she could understand it. To her it seemed so unbelievable that a man could wipe away sin by hanging on a cross. It didn't make any sense to her. There had to be someone she could talk to that could explain it to her better. The last person she wanted to ask was her sister, but she knew that was exactly what she needed to do. Her car seemed to head over there of its own volition. It seemed no matter how many times she told herself it was a bad idea, she still ended up outside of her sister's front door with her finger on the doorbell.

"Marguerite! I'm so glad you're here. I'm about to head out to prayer meeting. Come with me."

"Wait. What? No way."

"Yes way, I'm running late, but something kept me here. It must've been God keeping me here for you. Now we'd better hurry or we'll be late." She put her arm around Marguerite and led her to her minivan.

"I'm not so sure about this, sis."

"What's not to be sure about? You come, you

listen. If you like what you hear, maybe you come back. If you don't, well, that's a question for afterward."

"Fine. I guess." She hopped into the passenger seat and let her sister whisk her away to church.

When they left the meeting a little over an hour later, she had more questions than she'd started with. She drilled Florence on the way back to her house. "I have to think about this some more. I think I'm starting to understand, but it seems too grand for me to accept." She opened the passenger door and let herself out.

Flo got out of the car and joined her on the sidewalk. "I understand that. Let's go inside and talk. I have ice cream."

"Butter pecan?"

"No, but I have rocky road."

"Close second. I'll take it."

The two of them ambled inside and Flo's kids nearly knocked Marguerite over with hugs. Flo dished out ice cream for everyone and served the kids at the coffee table so they could talk in the kitchen. "I didn't understand and accept in one day either, sis. It took me months of searching. For some people, they hear the gospel once, they go down for the altar call and their life is never the same. For others, it's a journey, a search for the truth, but once you know, you know." She smiled. "I'm glad you're asking the questions."

"I don't think I would've been if it weren't for Diego." She took a bite of ice cream and savored the taste of the chocolate. Chocolate was supposed to heal anything, but she didn't think it could help her now.

"I know, but don't let a man stand in the way of your salvation. You can't do this for him, it has to be for you."

"Justine said the same thing."

"Trust us." She leaned back in her chair. "I didn't follow my own advice. It was years before Travis found Jesus, and those years were miserable. If I had it to do over again, I wouldn't have married him then." She shifted in her seat. "Of course, I'm glad we were married or we wouldn't have our three beautiful children and yes, it worked out in the end, but more often than not, marriages that begin like ours end in divorce."

"You think I'd make Diego miserable?"

"No. That's not it. God simply won't bless a marriage that doesn't have Him at its center."

"He hasn't asked me to marry him."

"And if he's following his faith, he won't unless and until you're saved."

"I get that. I guess, but it hurts." She pushed her bowl away. "I thought he could be the one. He seems perfect in every other way."

"Have a second helping of ice cream. I think you need it tonight. Don't forget to add some whipped cream."

Diego struggled with the heavy weight, while Chaz spotted for him. When the two finished weight training, they moved to the cardio area and took their places on treadmills.

"What are you doing, man?"

"Cardio. Isn't it the same thing you're doing?"

"I'm referring to the girl. What are you doing with her?"

"She's a woman."

"That doesn't answer my question."

"No. It doesn't."

"I don't think I'm wrong in guessing that Marguerite is not saved."

"No. She's not."

"Then, again, as your best friend, I must ask, what are you doing?"

"Falling in love."

"That's what I was afraid of. You've got to end it, man."

"I know."

"If you know, then why are you still seeing her?"

"I'm not sure I can explain it. I want so badly for her to be the one. I can see her as my wife. She's the whole package, Chaz."

"She's not the whole package if she's not saved. If you care about her, let her go, before you both wind up with hearts broken beyond repair."

"Easy for you to say. You already have the perfect woman, and now you're marrying into the Campos family. Could you ask for anything more?"

"She's marrying into the Smith family."

"You should take her last name. Campos is far better than Smith."

Chaz laughed. The two of them finished their workouts in companionable silence. When they were leaving the locker room, Chaz put his hand on Diego's shoulder. "I'm not usually one to interfere, but I don't want to see you jump head first off a cliff. Promise me you'll think about it, okay?"

"I will. I was thinking about it before we had this talk. I know what I have to do, but I hate it." He ran his fingers through his hair. "I want to be with her."

"I'm sorry, man. You'll get through this easier if you do it now then if you wait." Chaz gave him a friendly punch in the arm and walked away.

Back in his truck, images of Marguerite flooded his mind. How was he going to end his budding relationship with her? Why couldn't he have fallen for a woman who shared his faith? He'd known better than to get involved, but now here he was, trying to dig out carefully without setting off an avalanche of emotion.

CHAPTER 5

Diego picked Marguerite up after work and took her to the restaurant where they'd had their first date. She looked stunning in a simple black dress and heels. He would give nearly anything to make this woman his. He shoved aside the what-ifs and tried to enjoy the last bit of time they had together.

Dinner had been bittersweet. Knowing he had to end things with her was tearing him apart. He could tell by her body language that she knew it was over between them. His heart ached. He'd known better than to get involved, but the temptation had been overwhelming. Now, he wanted nothing more than to stay in this moment, so that they could remain together.

She was lovely, but it was more than looks that attracted him to her. It was her sense of humor, which she wore as a shield of armor. It was her sweet side. The way she'd allowed him a glimpse into her vulnerability the day they'd met when she'd expressed her concern for the wellbeing of the victims. It was her tough side. The way she'd struggled to make the SWAT team, which was an amazing feat of strength and endurance for any man, but especially admirable for a woman of her size. There wasn't much he didn't adore about her, but she didn't love Christ. And there was no way he could continue on with a woman who didn't share his faith. It was the only non-negotiable. Anything else, he would've tried to work through, but there was no way he'd marry a woman who didn't love Christ and there was no way he could continue spending time with Marguerite without their physical relationship progressing. For him that meant marriage. He wanted her more than anything else on earth, but he knew it wouldn't work.

He opened the passenger door and walked her to her door. They stood there staring into each other's eyes.

"I know you don't want to come in." She stumbled over the words.

"Oh, I want to, more than anything, but I won't."

"That's what I meant." She reached out and cupped the side of his face, still gazing into his eyes. She then stroked the stubble on his jawline with her knuckles. "Goodbye, Diego. I enjoyed these past few weeks and I wish they could continue, but now that I understand what your faith requires, I know we can't go on."

"You're breaking up with me?"

"Would you prefer I wait for you to break it off?"

He pulled her close and held her tightly. "I don't want to let you go."

"I don't want this either, but better now than in another week or month. Trust me, this is painful enough now."

When he pulled back and saw her tears it nearly undid him. After a sharp intake of breath, he wiped her tears away. "I wish things were different." He kissed her gently and took a step back.

"Me too."

She let herself into her house and he heard the key turn in the lock. It was another minute before he could bring himself to walk back to his car. She'd known what was coming and had relieved him of the responsibility of ending their relationship. It was her way of taking control of the situation and he understood that, but she was also saving him the pain of saying the words himself. As he drove away, he let himself cry, it was something he hadn't done since his father passed away.

***

Marguerite sat at her regular table. She usually enjoyed her weekly breakfast croissant. It was one of the few treats she allowed herself. Today it tasted like sandpaper. There was nothing wrong with the food, it was the ache in her heart causing her lack of enthusiasm for her meal. A few minutes of people watching didn't improve her mood. It seemed lovers surrounded her. At another table, a man wiped whipped cream from a woman's cheek. Near the front door, a girl kissed her boyfriend with gusto. Couples everywhere she looked. Where had they all come from? She tossed a tip on the table and scurried from the coffee shop.

Outside wasn't much better. A woman leaned against a nearby store front flirting with a guy in a cowboy hat. It was time to stop obsessing over Diego. This wasn't her style. She wasn't a boy crazy teenager. A fully grown woman with a seemingly perfect life did not obsess over a man. Maybe if she told herself that enough times, it would become true.

She strolled over to Florence's salon. She didn't usually show up without an appointment, but she needed to do something and talking with Flo felt right.

At the reception desk, she greeted Lisa. "I see you've changed from purple to green streaks. Fabulous new look."

Lisa's face lit up at the compliment. "Did you have an appointment, Mar? I don't see you in the book."

"I'm not in the book, I was hoping to catch up with my sister for her lunch break."

"Then you're in luck. She had a cancellation, so she'll have about forty-five minutes free and clear. Why don't you sit down a minute? I'll let her know you're here."

Ten minutes later, they tucked into a corner booth at the local diner.

"This was a pleasant surprise, Mar." Flo straightened the menus.

"I want to talk to you about this Jesus thing."

"This Jesus thing? Jesus isn't a thing, He's God."

"He is?"

"Yes. I have a homework assignment for you if you want to learn about Jesus."

"What's that?"

"I want you to read the gospel of John. You'll find it enlightening."

"Is it long?"

"No. It's only twenty-one chapters. You can easily read it tonight before bed."

"I'll read it."

"Good."

"In the meantime, will you help me understand what the hype is about?"

"I'd love to."

An hour later, she left her sister back at the

salon. Flo had gotten carried away telling her about Jesus and had lost track of time. She was late for her next client. On the drive home, Marguerite pondered the things Flo had explained. She'd shared her personal testimony, most of which Marguerite knew about, but she hadn't connected the change in her sister to Jesus. It hadn't occurred to her that the day she'd turned her life around was the day she'd accepted Christ. It was a lot to process.

When she arrived home, she pulled out a dusty copy of the King James Bible that she'd received as a gift from Brady years earlier. Turning to John she started reading. Sometime later, she took a break for dinner and considered what she'd read so far. If the book was true than what Flo said was accurate. Jesus was God. That helped explain why his sacrifice would be enough to wash away sin when a man's own sacrifices weren't. How could he be God and Man at the same time? It was too much to fathom. Maybe she wasn't meant to understand. Maybe it was enough to accept it. Could she accept something she couldn't fully grasp? Was it possible to fully grasp God? She opened the Bible to a random passage between bites of her fettuccine. The verse she read was in Isaiah.

> *For as the heavens are higher than the earth, so are my ways higher than your ways, and my thoughts than your*

thoughts.

It seemed like a direct answer to her questioning thoughts, but that was too fantastic for her to believe, so she put the thought aside. When she finished her dinner, she got comfortable on the couch and finished reading the gospel of John. She'd always considered the Bible too difficult to understand, but reading a whole book in order made it more accessible and easier to comprehend. She wondered why she'd always picked out individual verses here and there to read instead of reading it straight through from beginning to end like other books.

⁂

Being summoned to the governor's office annoyed Marguerite to no end. She couldn't understand why the governor felt the need to meddle in her life.

"Good morning, Marguerite." The governor had a firm handshake. "I'm glad you could stop by. Come in. Sit down."

When Marguerite perched on the edge of a chair, the governor took her seat behind the desk. It felt a little like being called to the principal's office.

"What can I do for you, Governor Campos?"

"I was sorry to hear about you and Diego. The two of you would've made a lovely match and I can only imagine how beautiful my grandchildren would've been, but I digress. I called you here to discuss your upcoming media tour."

"My media tour?"

"Yes, we need you to meet with the networks to talk about what it's like being the first female SWAT trooper. I know you'll do great." She handed Marguerite a list of media appointments.

"No way."

"This isn't a request, Marguerite. The appointments have been made. Your superiors have approved everything. This is happening."

"You don't want me to do this. I'll say the wrong things and embarrass the department and your campaign."

"Is that a threat?"

"No. It isn't a threat. It's the truth. I'm not a politician. You don't want me to play at being one."

"I trust that you'll do your best to make the department look praiseworthy. By doing so, you'll also make me look good. We're counting on you." Governor Campos stood, effectively dismissing her.

There was no stopping the sharp stabbing pain she felt when she saw Diego approaching. Attempting to keep her demeanor professional, she smiled. "Hello."

"Hi, Marguerite. I wasn't expecting to see you here."

"I was summoned to see your mother."

"Ah. I see." He ran his fingers through his thick hair. "It didn't go well?"

"No. It didn't. She booked a media tour."

"I'm sorry."

"Why? Did you tell her to set it up?"

"I did not. No."

"Then there isn't anything for you to be sorry about." She brushed past him and made her way to her car. Once safely inside, she let herself cry. She wasn't sure if the tears were due to the frustration of being forced to do something she wasn't equipped for or if they were over the man she'd been sure was her soul mate. Seeing him again brought up unresolved emotions, and the hole in her heart wasn't healing.

<hr>

The first week without Marguerite in his life left Diego feeling empty. Elena reminded him that if Christ was all he had than he was blessed beyond measure. He knew she was right, but the loss was painful and he mourned it. Again and again he chastised himself for getting involved in the first place. He'd known better. Falling for a non-believer was a mistake he couldn't afford to make, yet he'd gone in with his eyes wide open.

Over the following weeks, his heart began to heal. He spent more time in his Bible and in prayer, and stopped neglecting his personal Bible study, and even attended a couple of prayer meetings as his schedule allowed.

A couple of months after they'd ended their relationship, he ran into Marguerite outside of his mother's office, a supposedly chance meeting he was certain his mother had orchestrated. He'd felt his heart jump when he saw her. The pain that came was swift and sharp, but he was able to bear it. He'd spoken with briefly with her before she'd brushed past him. As he'd walked into his mother's lair, he'd felt Marguerite's eyes on him.

It was obvious she was hurting. He'd been such a fool. It was one thing to set himself up for heartache, but to do the same to an unsuspecting woman who didn't know anything about his faith or values was wrong.

One night at the shelter, Elena cornered him. "Enough."

"What?"

"Enough moping around. It's time you forgive yourself."

"I'm not sure I'm ready to do that."

"You don't think the blood of Jesus is enough?

You think you have to do some kind of penance in order to earn forgiveness?"

"You know perfectly well I'm not suggesting that."

"Then let it go. You messed up. Confess it and get over it."

"How exactly do I get over it?"

"Easily. Cast your cares upon Him."

"Sounds simple enough, but—"

"It is that simple. You only have to be willing." Elena walked away.

He was left standing there mouth open ready to keep arguing. Who was he arguing with anyway? Himself? God? It was time to let it go. Elena was right. And she knew it. It was obnoxious how she knew when she was right. Little sisters were supposed to get advice from their older brothers, yet his baby sister had wisdom beyond her years.

⚬

She sat down in the last pew. Something told her that today would change her forever. The thought both terrified and exhilarated her. Her usual punctuality hadn't failed her and she'd arrived while the choir still practiced. Her sister had asked her to save a seat. Flo was habitually tardy, so Marguerite assumed she'd get there sometime around the middle of service. She was pleasantly surprised when she'd arrived before the preacher made his way to the podium. "I thought you'd be later," she whispered.

Her sister smiled and hushed her children as she hustled them into the pew. At the end of the service the preacher did an altar call. She'd never seen one before except in the sappy movies her sister made her watch. It took until the preacher gave the third invitation before she got up the courage to make her way to the front. She found herself on her knees in front of the entire church sobbing hysterically. After the service, an older woman sat with her and the preacher and the two showed her from the Bible how to be saved.

When she left the service she felt lighter. A walking on air kind of light. Her sister hugged her with a strength and fierceness, clearly happy about Marguerite's profession of faith. She still had too many questions to list, but somehow she knew that everything was going to be okay. For once in her life, she wasn't counting on a man for her happiness. She'd found peace by accepting the gift Jesus had freely offered her. In one way it was humbling, not being able to earn her own salvation, but in another way it was freeing. Nothing else she'd done in her life had been as powerful as the simple choice she'd made that morning.

In the coming weeks and months, she attended church every chance she got. Rarely did she miss a Bible study or even a Sunday night service. Her commitment was unwavering. She even read her Bible from Genesis to Revelations for the first time. Brady explained that it was normal to thirst for knowledge after being saved. It was an exciting time in a new Christian's life; they'd been born-again, and as an infant learns so much in its first year, so must the baby Christian if they are to grow in their faith.

Marguerite paused at the door before knocking. Her stomach was twisted in knots, but even if volunteering for Elena's House of Hope turned out to be an awkward failure, she had to try. The women she'd committed to deserved to be put before her own insecurities.

Elena opened the door with a huge smile. "I'm so glad you could make it, Marguerite. The women have been looking forward to this since I told them you were coming."

"Really?"

"Yes, most of them have never taken self-defense classes and to have a real SWAT trooper come in and teach them is amazing." She wrinkled up her brow. "One of the ladies we took to the shelter in California disappeared last night, Maria. Do you remember her?"

Marguerite nodded.

"We're hoping she left of her own free will, but something tells me she didn't."

"You think there was foul play?"

"Diego doesn't. He says she probably left on her own, but I'm not so sure. Only the FBI and our volunteers know where that shelter is, so the chances of her being abducted from there are slim, but I'm not comfortable with her disappearance."

"It's disturbing."

"It is. It's more reason for the ladies to learn self-defense."

"I'll second that."

"Follow me." Elena pulled open a door leading to a staircase. "We're going to hold the class in the rec room, so that everyone has room to maneuver."

Once downstairs, Marguerite took note of the ten women sitting in a circle around the room. She was early, but they were ready for her. "Well, since you're ready, why don't we get started a few minutes early?"

Sounds of approval followed, so she continued. "I'm going to need a volunteer."

None of the women volunteered, so Elena stepped up. Marguerite demonstrated some basic moves for getting out of holds. One by one the women took turns helping her demonstrate moves. She showed them an open hand strike and had them try it on her. Following that, they tried a knee kick. Once they got through the basics, she had them pair up and she and Elena demonstrated each move, before the ladies practiced the moves on each other.

After the lesson, she spoke, "These moves are great for getting out of trouble once you're in it. The best defense is ultimately prevention. Always be aware of your surroundings. Walk with a purpose and know where you're going. Keep your key in your hand as you approach your car. If someone tries to take your purse or wallet, it's better to give it to them than it is to fight, your life is worth more than a few dollars. Always make noise if someone approaches you. Don't obey the attacker when they tell you to be quiet. Scream.

"I know that telling women to be smart about the situations they put themselves in comes across as victim blaming, but it's not. It's proactively ensuring your own safety. When a woman is attacked it is not her fault for not being careful enough, it's the attackers fault and only his fault, but that will come as little comfort to parents mourning the loss of their daughter. Stay safe out there."

After the lesson, she was invited to stay for the evening snack. Elena sat beside her at the long table. "Thanks for coming tonight."

"I'm glad to do it."

"I was afraid you wouldn't want to volunteer with me after what happened between you and Diego."

"If I'm being honest, I was nervous about coming."

"There is no reason we can't be friends, right?" Elena asked.

"No. There isn't." Marguerite grinned. "I admire what you do with the ladies and I hope we can be friends."

"He misses you, you know?"

"I didn't know, but I know I miss him."

"Sorry, I shouldn't have brought him up when we were having a perfectly lovely evening. My sincere apologies. Let's talk about the weather."

"Those flash floods were disastrous," Marguerite said.

"Yes! They took out some RVs. I heard two people were still missing."

"I hope they find them alive."

"Me too. I've been praying," Elena said.

Marguerite had joined the choir as a way to get involved. She enjoyed singing, and she soon learned that the hymns they sang were powerful and deep. It was an honor to be able to raise her voice to God in song. They practiced on Monday evenings and Saturday afternoons. One such Saturday, she was singing "Redeemed" when Diego walked through the door. She nearly fell off the platform. He stood staring at her as if seeing her for the first time. She hurried down to greet him. "Were you looking for me?"

"No. I didn't expect to see you here. I'm um. I came to see Pastor Dan. We're having lunch."

"I didn't know you attended this church. I've haven't seen you here before."

"I don't. Not usually. I go to a church closer to home. Pastor Dan and I are old friends."

"Oh. That's nice."

"I'm shocked to see you here, Marguerite."

"I would've called you, but it was explained to me that I needed to put my 'budding' faith first."

"You have wise friends. I can't begin to tell you how happy it makes me to see you here."

"I think I'm starting to understand," she said.

"Praise the Lord."

"I better get back up there."

"Okay."

She walked back to the front of the church.

"Is it okay if I call you?" he shouted.

She beamed and turned to face him. "I'd love that."

Her thoughts were consumed with him for the rest of practice, and she kept messing up.

Approaching the reception desk, Marguerite grinned. "Bright red highlights. They're unexpected, Lisa, but as pretty as the green."

"Thanks, Mar. I'll buzz Flo for you, she's in the back stocking the supplies they delivered this morning."

Flo came out with scissors in hand. "You ready for that trim?"

"He called."

"Who called?"

"Diego."

"Wait. I thought you hadn't heard from him in months."

"I hadn't, but I ran into him at church choir practice a few days ago."

"Back up. What was he doing at church choir practice? Wait come to my station and you can tell me while I cut."

She followed Flo and sat down in the swivel chair. "He came by to pick Pastor Dan up for lunch. They're apparently friends."

"Oh. Interesting."

"I'll bet he was surprised to see you."

"I'm not sure a fork-lift would've been able to pick his jaw up off the floor."

"Wow. So, the phone call?"

"He asked if he could call me. I wasn't sure what I was supposed to say, but I said yes."

"And he called."

"He did. It took him a few days, so I didn't think he was going to call."

"What was his excuse?"

"He wanted to pray about it first."

"Well, I can't fault him for that."

"He doesn't think it was a coincidence that we ran into each other. He wants to take me out tonight."

"I assume you're going?"

"Of course I'm going."

"You're in love with him."

"I didn't say that."

"You didn't have to. I thought it before you two broke off your relationship, but now I'm sure. It's so obvious."

"I'm crazy about him, yes, but I don't know about love."

"You'll realize it soon enough."

Chapter 6

At Diego's request, Marguerite had dressed casually, but still wanted to look her best, so she'd changed her clothes several times before settling on a cute outfit she thought he would like. Spritzing her perfume, she walked through the mist, and then took her time carefully applying her makeup. She wanted everything to be perfect. She couldn't contain her excitement. They were getting a second chance, and she wanted to make the most of it.

When he finally arrived, she stepped out of the way to invite him in. He joined her in the living room. Shadow rubbed up against his leg, confirming for her that he was indeed perfect. Shadow didn't like men and didn't bond with them, so the tabby's behavior bewildered and pleased Marguerite.

Diego startled her when he bent down and kissed her. She leaned in to the kiss and drew closer to him.

"We should get going," Diego said.

"Old habits die hard. We're getting the slightest bit intimate and you're running away."

"Not running away. You have no idea how badly I want to do more than kiss you, Mar. But I intend to make you mine first."

She wondered what he meant by that, but didn't ask. "Let me grab my purse. Then we can be on our way."

Diego stood and grabbed her before she could leave the room. He pushed her against the wall and kissed her with more passion then he'd ever shown. When he finally broke the contact, his breathing was ragged. "I'll wait outside," he said.

Deep breathing didn't help slow her racing heart. At least now she understood why he'd stopped. It didn't make it easier to live with, but now she wanted their relationship to be God honoring also. She could accept a slower pace than she was used to if it meant that they would please God.

He took her to the same ice cream shop where they'd shared burgers and cones. "I want to start over, so I thought visiting some of the same places would be a way to renew our relationship. This time putting God first."

"It's a splendid idea, but how are you going to get that fawn back here?" she asked.

"Sorry, I'm not that good."

"Thank you."

"For what?" he asked.

"For bringing me here again. It's perfect."

"You nearly killed me back at your place."

"What do you mean?" She batted her eyelashes playfully and twirled her hair.

"You know perfectly well what I mean." He took the cone from her hand and captured her lips again. By the time he returned her cone, it was a soggy mess, but she didn't care. She wanted nothing more than to melt into him and stay there for the long haul.

"I'm sorry I walked away." With one hand on the steering wheel, Diego reached over and took Marguerite's left hand in his.

"Don't be." Marguerite scooted closer and leaned into him while he drove. "I might not have found Jesus if you hadn't. Besides, I broke up with you, remember?"

"Semantics." He stopped the truck and turned toward her. "You were being merciful."

"Maybe." Her eyes misted over. "It tore me apart at first, but I learned how to be content by myself. With God, I mean, but without a man beside me. As much as I missed you, I think in the end it will make me a better companion."

"You're beautiful." He ran his knuckles across her jaw line. "Inside and out."

"You've said that before, but I won't tire of hearing it." She put her hand over his. "Are we going to sit in the truck forever?"

"No. Let's get out and walk." He helped her out and then threaded his fingers through hers, leading her along the path that ran beside the river. "Do you remember when we came here?"

"I do." She smiled. "It was one of our first dates."

"Yes." He grinned and reached into his pocket. "I thought it would be the perfect place—" He pulled his phone from his pocket. "My phone. It's work. This can't wait. Do you mind riding along?"

"Will you at least finish your sentence first? The perfect place for what?"

"We'll have to get back to that later. It's that serial killer case I've been working on."

"Did I know you were working on a serial killer case?"

He took her hand in his again and headed back toward the truck. "It's what led us to that raid where we met."

"I didn't know anything about that."

He spent the twenty minute drive filling her in on the details. When they arrived, they joined the medical examiner at the scene. "Harper, you got here quickly."

"I was in the morgue when I got the call and it's only a ten minute drive," Dr. Walsh said.

He introduced Marguerite and Harper.

"It's nice to meet you, Marguerite. Wish it were under better circumstances."

"Sorry about the attire." Diego glanced down at his shorts. "We were on a casual date."

"No problem. Glad you're here. The witnesses were freaking out, so I sent them inside to wait on the sheriff. When he called he said he was going to text you, but that it'd be at least thirty minutes before he could get here."

"Is he sending a deputy?"

"He said he would, but didn't sound confident about them getting here quickly."

"What do we have here? Same MO?"

"Exactly the same. Except the dump site is much more public."

"My guess is we missed a body dump and he's aggravated, so he dumped this one in a public place." He scratched at the stubble growing in on his chin.

"Nobody should die like that. She was discarded like a piece of rubbish." Marguerite stared down at the woman's mutilated body noticing the number branded on her left ankle.

Diego put his hand on her shoulder. "Why don't you wait by the truck? You don't need to be any more involved in this than you already are."

"No. It's fine. I'll stay here. Tell me what I can do to help."

"Officially, nothing. You're not on this case, but you may be able to calm the witnesses inside the diner."

"Sure thing." Marguerite strode inside with a confidence he wished he had when dealing with witnesses.

Marguerite scooted close to Diego on the ride home. "Dr. Harper Walsh has a thing for you."

"You may be correct, darling."

"Why aren't you dating her?"

"Because I'm dating you."

"Is that the only reason?"

"One of many," he said.

"Which are?"

"For one, she works with dead bodies, willingly."

"So do you."

"Not all day. Not every day."

"Okay, I can see how that would be a strike

against her, but it would be countered by the fascinating stories she must have to tell."

I'll give you that, and at first I thought about overlooking her choice of career, but we were working a case together, so I didn't think I should take her out. Later, there was another woman on my mind. Taking up most of my time and energy."

"And who would that be?"

"I don't think you need to ask."

"Should I be jealous? She was eying you up like a lion does an antelope." Marguerite turned in the seat so she could better read his features. "She's a knockout."

"Yes. She is, but she's not the woman sitting beside me, is she?"

"That's what I'm trying to figure out. Why would you be out with me, when you could be out with her?"

"Because I chose you." He grinned. "I could turn this around on you, you know."

"How so?"

"I've seen the way Seth Jacobs looks at you."

"He does not look at me in any way other than as a subordinate member of his SWAT team."

"You don't think so, huh?" He laughed. "Clearly, you know very little about the male species and what it looks like when a man is attracted to a woman."

"You're crazy."

"Am I?" He pulled into her driveway and got out of the truck. When he opened her door, he held out his hand to assist her. Once inside the house, he drew her into his arms. "I think I know how a man acts when he's attracted to you, mi tesoro."

She leaned her face toward his. "Maybe you should show me."

His kiss was sweet and gentle. "Maybe we should forget about how Seth looks at you and how Harper looks at me and instead concentrate on how we look at each other."

"That's a marvelous idea." Marguerite ran her finger down his neck and along his collar bone. Then she followed the same trail with her lips.

Diego groaned. "You're trying to kill me."

"Would I do that?"

"You've been doing that since we met."

She smiled coyly and took a step back. "Do you think you can keep your hands to yourself long enough to watch a movie tonight?"

"That's rich." He chuckled. "I should ask you the same." He kissed her again. "I'd love to stay and watch a movie, if that's what you're offering."

Having Diego in her living room with the lights dim and the movie on was a test of her self-control. She knew she had to behave and watch the movie, but he wasn't helping matters. Whenever she began to become engrossed in the movie, he would lean down and kiss her neck and the sensation of his stubble against her skin would cause her to lose her concentration.

When she walked him to the door that night, they said an extended goodbye, then as he was leaving, she grabbed his hand to keep him from leaving. "You didn't finish telling me what the trail beside the river was a perfect place for?"

"No. I didn't. And now, you'll have to wait until we can get back there again."

"That isn't fair."

"Life's not fair, mi tesoro."

Marguerite flipped the pancakes while she watched Florence simultaneously fry bacon, control a sibling rivalry, and set the table.

"How do you do it, sis?"

"Do what?"

She gestured around the room. "This. All of it. Keep the kids from killing each other, get breakfast on the table, work as a full-time stylist, and run the business end of your shop."

"The first female SWAT Trooper is asking me how I do what I do. That's rich."

"I'm serious. I think it's easier to storm warehouses and bust meth labs then to do what you do."

"Believe me, it becomes second nature. It isn't easy, but you get used to it."

"I'm not sure I'm buying it."

"Then you're a smart woman. You don't get used to it." Flo laughed. Then she flipped the bacon before bending down to remove a foreign object from her toddler's mouth. "It's a good thing they're so cute. God made them adorable, so we wouldn't throttle them."

Marguerite put the tray of pancakes on the table and set out the butter and syrup.

"What time is Diego picking you up?"

"He's not. I told him I'd meet him there."

"Is that your escape plan? You'll have your car, so you can get away?"

"Maybe. The last time I saw his mother, I may have come off a little abruptly."

"You think? You told me about the conversation. She was out of line, but—"

"But I should've played nice. Yeah. I know."

"Try to relax. Elena will be there. She's sure to be an ally."

"I think so, yes. She takes issue with her mother's aggressiveness."

Flo hollered for everyone to come to the table and they sat down. Flo's husband, Travis, said grace before they dug into the food.

———————

Dinner at the governor's house wasn't exactly what Marguerite had expected. Apparently, Estelle Campos and her children knew how to unwind. They drank soda, ate take-out pizza, and enjoyed relaxed conversation. At first, the governor didn't appear inclined to mention their last conversation or Marguerite's poor attitude about the press tour. She was grateful for the reprieve. Although, she expected to have to swallow her pride and apologize, she didn't want to address it in front of the others.

Later, when Marguerite meandered into the kitchen to fill her soda glass, Diego's mother cornered her. "Marguerite, may I speak with you for a moment."

"Sure." Marguerite leaned against the island in the center of the kitchen and waited for her to continue.

"I owe you an apology."

"No. I should apologize. I was out of line the last time we met," Marguerite said.

"You were a bit terse, but I blame myself." She made eye contact. "I should've consulted you before setting up the media tour. It was presumptuous of me."

"Thank you for saying that."

"I believe it was the proper thing for you to do, and I'm glad you comported yourself well during the interviews, but if I had it to do over again, I would've handled it with more tact and conferred with you beforehand."

"Thank you, Governor."

"Please call me Estelle."

"Okay. Although that might take some getting used to."

"It seems you and my son are getting serious and I can't have you calling me 'governor' over Sunday dinners."

Marguerite laughed, but then got serious. "May I ask you something?"

Estelle leaned back against the counter. "Go ahead."

"When I ran into Diego at your office a few months back, was that orchestrated?"

"Yes. It was. He was so unhappy. I thought if I told you both to be at my office within a twenty minute interval, you might 'accidentally' run into each other." She pushed herself away from the counter. "I know it was foolish, but a mother abhors seeing her son suffer. I'd hoped you two might mend fences."

"I can understand that."

"Shall we get back in there before Diego sends out a search party?"

"He would too," Marguerite said.

The conversation had left her feeling lighter.

After a rambunctious game of charades with his family, Diego walked Marguerite to her car. "I'll follow you."

"Don't you have work tomorrow?"

"I do, but we have a little more time. Maybe we can sit on your screen porch and listen to the sounds of the night?"

"I'd like that." In truth, she was thrilled to get some alone time with him.

CHAPTER 7

It had been another rough couple of days with the discovery of the fourth body, but the BAU was tracking down leads and had made suggestions on leads for him to follow. He was ready to begin fresh using their profile to help him narrow down the list of possible suspects.

Diego sorted through the list of possible suspects generated by the FBI analysts from data found on the laptop. It wasn't much to go on, and the chance that the perp was in that list was slim, but it was a start. Painstakingly, he combed through printed data while Agent Angelo Mertz searched computer files. Mertz had been assigned to fill in for Tom. The problem was that he liked to talk. He chattered on about baseball while Diego attempted to concentrate. Every few minutes, he would throw out another stat. It seemed he was as obsessed with baseball as Tom was with health fads.

About three hours into the search, Mertz interrupted him again. "I know you said to stop talking, but I think you might be interested in this."

"What's that?"

"You know that letter you got at the first scene you were called out to?"

"The one the deputy ran down for me?"

"Yes, that one."

"What about it?"

"You got that second letter and it was similar, but the reporter's elimination prints were the only ones on it."

"True."

"From what we got from the profilers, that reporter, Jason Blake, fits the profile exactly."

Diego sat back in the chair and picked up a copy of the profile, reading the bullet points aloud.

- *Caucasian male,*
- *In his late twenties to early thirties,*
- *May be married with children,*
- *Intelligent,*
- *Professional with a college degree,*
- *Inserts himself into the investigation, and*
- *Believes he's smarter than everyone around him.*

Diego headed out to question the reporter with Agent Mertz. The gated community in which Jason Blake lived seemed to be a bit above his pay grade, but he wasn't sure how much journalists earned, so he tucked the thought away to explore later. Angelo walked slightly behind him as he approached the front door.

"Hello, Mr. Blake. We had a few more questions with regard to that note you received."

The man welcomed him with a smile. "Sure. I'm happy to help in any way I can." He stiffened and a look of unease settled on his face when he noticed Agent Mertz.

"Do you two know each other?" Diego asked.

Diego felt the barrel of a gun press against the back of his head. How did he not realize Mertz was the killer, he fit the profile every bit as much as Jason Blake did. He'd volunteered for this assignment when Tom had been injured, thus injecting himself into the investigation. Maybe even before that. Hadn't he brought the warrant? How had he gotten involved in that? Had Tom called him? His blood boiled. Mertz had run down his partner in cold blood. He should've known something was off about Angelo Mertz that day when he'd brought that warrant. He'd stayed back and watched the action unfold like a disinterested moviegoer watching a scene unfold on the big screen, not someone who was in the middle of a real life human trafficking bust.

Mertz had shown no warmth. No heart.

He wondered if he'd ever get the chance to ask Marguerite to marry him. Why had he put it off? Maybe he could keep Mertz talking and distract him until help arrived, but there wasn't much hope of helping coming. The houses were on substantial lots, the development had been well-designed to prevent neighbors from disturbing each other. They'd shown their credentials at the gatehouse, so nobody would know to send help. "What are you doing, Mertz?"

"I'm setting Blake up to take the fall for the killings and he's going to shoot you as you attempt to arrest him for the murders. I'll be the hero that tried to save your life. I'll take out a serial killer in the process. It's rather brilliant if I may say so myself." His hand was steady as he held the Glock.

"Isn't that your department issued Glock? How are you going to explain that away?" Diego asked.

"Blake managed to take it from me in the midst of the struggle. Your death was an unpreventable tragedy."

"Tell me about the note?" Diego took a step inside when Angelo pushed him in that direction. "Why the note?"

"The first one was to taunt you." Angelo gave a lighthearted laugh. "But I soon realized I could use it to my advantage and set up a reporter. I took the report from the profilers, it was simple enough to find a patsy that fit the profile. I handed him the note personally, dressed as a courier."

"How did you avoid video surveillance?"

"I'm not stupid. I waited for him outside the building and played the fan. I told him I recognized him from his nightly newscast. I gave him the delivery and hurried away before he opened it."

"What about the brands? Why did you brand the women?"

"Mostly for fun, but it was a nifty way to identify them. No names, just numbers.

"You're sick." Diego could tell Mertz wanted to keep bragging, and figured it was the only thing keeping him alive, so he taunted him. "There is no way you'll get away with this."

"Wait and see. Oh yeah, you won't be around to see, but you can trust me. I'll get away with this, and I'll be the hero who tried in vain to save you." He fired the Glock. Diego fell to the ground. He could sense the blood seeping from the wound in his side, but was powerless to stop it; his vision went black around the edges before fading out completely.

Marguerite stared out the window as flashes of lightening lit up the sky. She was in the van with the rest of the SWAT team. There were only five of them now that Bob and José had been assigned to other teams. They were returning from a meth lab bust. Maricopa County disbanded their SWAT team, so they'd been called out often.

Seth took a call before switching seats with Marcus, so he could sit beside her. He leaned toward her and spoke in a near whisper. "I need to know if you can keep your head in the game. We don't have much time to switch troopers, but if we're able to get someone to the scene, we'll make a switch on location."

"Why would I need to be switched out? What's going on?"

"We got a case from the headquarters."

"And?"

"They got a call from the wife of nightly newscaster, Jason Blake. She arrived home and pulled into her garage. After hearing some commotion, she left her garage by an outside door and peered in a front window. She saw her husband and another individual being held at gunpoint. She gave headquarters the plate of the SUV on scene. It belongs to the FBI. The vehicle is assigned to Diego Campos. We don't know it it's him or his partner being held at gunpoint."

"His partner is on light duty. He's been working with another guy. I think the last name was Mertz."

"She had view of the gunmen, her husband, and one other man, but I can't tell you if was Mertz or Campos."

"We need to get both of them out of there."

"I'm hoping you'll be relieved from duty the moment we get there. I can see no good coming from you entering a house where your boyfriend may be being held at gunpoint."

"I'm on this team and I have more at stake than anyone else, so I will perform at my best."

"If I bring you in on this, I hope you're able to do just that." He sighed. "You need to prepare yourself for the worst. We may not be in time to save them."

"How far is it?"

"We're pulling into the development now, but Mrs. Blake called headquarters nine minutes ago." He met her stare. "That's a lot of time in a situation like this. Quite possibly, too much time."

She swallowed the lump in her throat and lowered her face shield. If it was her in there, she was sure Diego would do everything in his power to bring her out alive. The realization of how much she loved him hit her hard. She couldn't lose him after all they'd been through.

The other SWAT team hadn't arrived when they got to the scene, so Jacobs didn't make her sit it out. He did keep her with him where he could keep an eye on her. She stuck to his six as three of them rushed in through the garage. The other two SWAT troopers entered through the back door. There was no sign of Mrs. Blake in the garage. When they had a visual through the kitchen, they could see that Mrs. Blake had been tied to a chair with duct tape. Her husband was on his knees beside her. Diego was bleeding a few feet from them. She had to get to him.

On Jacobs' command, all five SWAT troopers moved into position and surrounded the assailant with their assault rifles pointed at him. The man aimed his gun at Jacobs and the rifles surrounding him fired at the same time. He fell to the floor, but didn't stop moving he raised his gun again and a shot to his head ended it.

Marguerite dropped to the floor by Diego's side. She checked his pulse and then whispered more to herself than anyone else, "He's alive."

Seth knelt beside the perpetrator and checked for life. "His vest didn't save him from the head shot. He's gone."

She put her hand on the wound in Diego's side in an attempt to stop the bleeding. "You're going to be fine," she said the words more to herself then to him. He had to be okay. There was no other acceptable outcome. She could hear the sirens outside. The ambulance had arrived. Lifting her head, she shouted "He needs an EMT."

<hr>

Marguerite strolled along the riverbank her hand in Diego's larger one. It had taken months for him to recover from his gunshot wound, but now he was able to walk with her again, and she'd never felt more alive. She pulled her hand from his, put her arm around his waist, and leaned into his side. "That day at Jason Blake's house, I thought I might lose you."

"I know," he said

"Don't ever do that to me again."

"I can't make any promises."

She stopped walking and stepped out in front of him. Meeting his gaze she held his hands in hers. "You know I love you, right?"

"I thought so. If you didn't love me this moment might get awkward." He dropped to a knee and pulled a box from his pocket. Opening the lid, so she could see the brilliant diamond inside, he asked, "Marguerite, I love you and want to spend the rest of my life with you. Will you marry me?"

"Yes! I will." She held out her left hand and he slid the ring onto her finger. A tear escaped and slid down her cheek.

He stood and put his hands on her shoulders. "If you love me why are you crying?"

"They're happy tears."

"I'll never understand women."

"Kiss me." Putting her arms around his neck, she stood on her tiptoes and kissed him. He kissed her senseless. After several minutes, she pulled back slightly. "When do you want to get married?"

"How about today? We could drive to Vegas."

"You're dreaming if you think I'm giving up my fantasy wedding for an Elvis impersonator."

"I wasn't serious, but the sooner the better." He placed a kiss on the bridge of her nose. "I've wanted to make you mine since the moment we met, mi tesoro, and I'm looking forward to the honeymoon."

EXCERPT OF LAWFULLY GUARDED

By Elle E. Kay

CHAPTER 1

When Alexander Whitaker's office door opened, Trenton Prescott turned his back on the spectacular view of the Pacific Ocean to face the woman entering the room. Her thick brown hair spilled down her back in waves, skimming her waistline. The picture he'd been sent of her didn't do her justice.

Interest sparked in her dark eyes as she looked him up and down. The mini dress she wore showed off her shapely legs, and he fought to keep his gaze on her face.

Delaney Whitaker lowered herself into the chair facing her father's mahogany desk. "What was it you wanted, Daddy?"

"I'd like you to meet Trenton Prescott of Garrison Security."

She turned and appraised him once more before offering her hand, which he shook. "Charmed, I'm sure."

Mr. Whitaker scowled at her. "Trent will be your bodyguard until such time when Courtney is safely returned home and I determine that the danger is past."

The woman sneered. "I will not be followed around like a child with a nanny."

"You will do exactly what you're told if you'd like to stay in my good graces, my dear." He leaned back in his chair, turning his stare from Delaney back to Trent. "Thank you for getting here so quickly. I appreciate everything Garrison Security is doing to help us during this difficult time."

"Glad to be of service, sir." Trent stood. "If we're about done here, I'd like to get going."

"I think we've covered everything," Mr. Whitaker stood and gave Trent a firm handshake.

The young woman rose to her feet, and the older man kissed the top of his daughters head, saluted Trent, and left him to face his surly client.

"Well, come on then." Delaney held the door open. "I'll get the staff to ready a room for you."

"We're not staying here." He brushed past her, and the sweet smell of jasmine tickled his nose.

"I'm not leaving home."

He turned to face her. "You don't have a say in the matter, princess. Your father and I worked out the details." He grinned. "You're not safe. Not even in your daddy's Bel Air mansion."

"We have excellent security."

"Yes. So excellent someone managed to get around security, turn off all the cameras, and kidnap your sister."

"My sister is a nitwit."

"Even so, you're coming with me."

"Where are we going?"

"We're staying in a safe-house outside of Seattle."

"Oh joy." She frowned. "My sister is in Seattle, so that's something, anyway." He didn't bother to tell her that she wouldn't see much of her sister while she was there.

He followed her through the state-of-the-art home, walking past a home theater, a wellness center, and a wine room. It would be a challenge for this pampered princess to live with him in a safe-house, no matter how well-appointed it was. When they finally arrived on the fourth level and traversed their way to Delaney's bedroom, he stood outside her door while she packed some things. She came out laden with enough luggage for a one month junket to Europe.

She dropped her bags at her feet and turned to a screen built into the wall. She pressed a button. "I'll need someone to bring my bags out, please."

A man's voice came through the speaker. "Right away, Miss Whitaker."

"I can carry your bags." Trent offered.

"How will you protect me with your hands full, Mr. Bodyguard?" Her words were spoken with seductive undertones. He might've been imagining it, but he didn't think so.

As they passed through the house on their way to the motor court, he admired the infinity pool through the glass on the west side of the house. The house felt more like a pricey hotel than a personal home to him.

⸙

Trent assisted Delaney out of the Escalade and onto Garrison Security's private jet, following her inside. She immediately went to the back of the plane where there was a small desk with a mirror. It resembled a make-up table although it was designed as a place for the staff to work away from the main area. He stood discreetly by watching as she reapplied her lipstick and brushed her hair.

When she finally rose to her feet and started back toward the seating area, she spotted him and raised an eyebrow. "Where are my things?"

"The staff loaded your luggage while you spent thirty minutes perfecting your lipstick."

"I did no such thing."

"Maybe it was closer to ten minutes, but you were definitely staring into that mirror back there with a lipstick in your hand."

She settled into one of the luxurious white leather seats. "You were spying on me?"

"I'm your bodyguard." He relaxed into the seat facing hers, stretching his long legs out on either side of hers. "I'm paid to watch you."

"So, that means you must observe me at all times? Even when I'm applying my lipstick?"

"It means when I'm on duty, I will not take my eyes off of you, unless you are in the privy."

"I didn't put makeup on to look good for you." She inspected her perfectly manicured nails.

"Of course not." He chuckled. "We're going to be around many other people on this private jet." He looked around the empty plane pointedly.

"The pilot might be cute."

"I'm sure her husband thinks so."

Her lips formed a pout and he fought the urge to laugh. Delaney Whitaker was going to be a handful.

"When you're not kidnapping billionaires' daughters, what do you do for fun, Mr. Prescott?"

"Call me Trent, but do you think jokes about kidnapping are appropriate considering the circumstances?"

She blushed. "I wasn't thinking."

He nodded, acknowledging her chagrin, but not making a big thing of it. "My job is what I do for fun." He gave her his most charming smile. "What could be more entertaining than watching young women melt down when they realize their freedom is being restricted?"

Ignoring the jab, she tossed her hair over her shoulder. "You must guard men and children, as well."

"Most of the time I guard men, yes. Occasionally I guard children." He stretched. "Unfortunately, I drew the short stick this time."

"You think you're hilarious, don't you?"

"You don't?" He grinned.

"I think you're annoying."

"Would you like a book to read?" He took a copy of *Pride and Prejudice* out of the cabinet beside him and held it out to her. "You don't have to waste your time conversing with the staff."

She didn't take the book. "Thanks anyway, but I think I'd rather annoy you."

"Lovely." He set down the book and loosened his tie. "I suppose I should get comfortable then."

"Tell me about yourself, Trent."

"There's not much to tell."

"I'm not sure I believe that." She raised an eyebrow. "How did you come to work for Garrison Security?"

It was an innocent enough question, but, if he wasn't careful, the explanation would tell her much more than he wanted to reveal. "Grayson Garrison and I were in the same unit."

"Unit? As in military?"

"Yes."

"Oh." She flipped her hair over her shoulder. "Did you see combat?"

Visions of war flashed before his eyes. "Yes." He felt a muscle jump in his jaw.

"I can see it's a sore subject."

"It is."

"Let's talk about something else. Tell me about your family."

"My family is great." A genuine smile played at the corners of his mouth. "My father is a real estate developer, and my mother works at his company."

"Any siblings?"

"No. I'm an only child."

"I suppose you never had to fight for affection."

"No, but I would've liked to have a sibling to commiserate with."

"It's not all it's cracked up to be."

"Why not?"

"I love my sisters, but we fought constantly growing up."

"I've heard that is usually the case." He stretched. "What about your parents? I met your father, but what happened to your mother."

"She died when I was young."

"I'm sorry."

"I barely remember her, but thank you." She smiled. "Daddy tells us wonderful stories."

He frowned. "I can't imagine growing up without a mother."

"My father played both roles to the best of his ability. Enough about me, where did you grow up?"

"Pennsylvania."

"Wow. Living in California must be so different from where you grew up."

"It would be." He leaned forward. "But, I don't live in California."

"Where do you live?"

"Maryland."

"Oh. I assumed you were a local."

"I can live anywhere with my work, but I choose to live near Garrison Security's headquarters."

"Would you ever consider relocating?"

"If circumstances dictated it, then yes."

She leaned back in her seat and closed her eyes. It gave him a chance to study her. Her exquisite beauty was unusual, even a bit exotic. It was a shame she was so far out of his league. Not that it mattered, since she didn't appear to share his values. Yet, there was something about Delaney Whitaker that made him hope to get to know her better.

Purchase a copy of *Lawfully Guarded* at your favorite retailer to read more.

Reader Letter

Dear Reader,

I hope you enjoyed reading *Lawfully Defended.* Please check out some of my other titles.

I'd love it if you'd sign up for my newsletter at: https://www.elleekay.com/newsletter-sign-up/.

If you enjoyed *Lawfully Defended,* the most helpful thing you can do is leave an honest review. So, please consider submitting a review on Amazon and/or GoodReads. It doesn't cost anything other than a moment of your time and can be tremendously beneficial to me. Your quick review helps to get my book into the hands of other readers who may enjoy it.

Amazon:
www.ElleEKay.com/readerlinks/777362

Goodreads:
www.ElleEKay.com/readerlinks/777362

For a list of my current books and upcoming releases check out the novel page on my website: https://www.elleekay.com/novels/

Thank you.

Elle E. Kay

https://www.elleekay.com

About Elle E. Kay

Elle E. Kay lives in the Back Mountain area of Pennsylvania. She loves life in the country on her hobby farm. Elle is a born-again Christian with a deep faith and love for the Lord Jesus Christ. She desires to live for Him and to put Him first in everything she does.

She writes children's books under the name Ellie Mae Kay.

You can connect with Elle on her website and blog at https://www.elleekay.com/ or on social media:

Facebook:
https://www.facebook.com/ElleEKay7

Twitter: https://twitter.com/ElleEKay7

Pinterest:
https://www.pinterest.com/elleekay7/

Amazon Author Central:
http://www.amazon.com/author/ellekay

Instagram:
https://www.instagram.com/elleekay7/

Goodreads:
https://www.goodreads.com/author/show/150
16833.Elle_E_Kay

I'd love it if you'd sign up for my newsletter at https://www.elleekay.com/newsletter-sign-up/

Acknowledgements

I would like to express my gratitude to my husband, Joe, for putting up with the long hours of writing and editing.

This story is a product of my imagination and a work of fiction. Names, characters, businesses, places, events, locales, and incidents are either the products of my imagination or in the case of actual towns, historical persons, and companies mentioned, they have been used in a fictitious manner. Any resemblance to actual persons, living or dead, or actual events is purely coincidental.

Any errors or deficiencies are my own.

Personal Testimony

I first came to know Jesus as a young teen, but before long I strayed from God and allowed my selfish desires to rule me. I sought after acceptance and love from my peers, not knowing that only God could fill my emptiness. My teen years were full of angst and misery, for me and my family. People I loved were hurt by my selfishness. My heartache was at times overwhelming, but I couldn't find the healing I desperately desired. After several runaway attempts my family was left with little choice, and they put me in a group home/residential facility where I would get the constant supervision I needed.

At that home I met a godly man called 'Big John' who tried once again to draw me back to Jesus. He would point out Matthew 11:28-30 and remind me that all I had to do to find peace was give my cares to Christ. I wanted to live a Christian life, but something kept pulling me away. The cycle continued well into adulthood. I would call out to God, but then I would turn away from Him. (If you read the old-testament you'll see that the nation of Israel had a similar pattern, they would call out to God and He would heal them and bring them back into their land.

Then they would stray and He would chastise them. It was a cycle that went on and on).

When I came to realize that God's love was still available to me despite all my failings, I found peace and joy that have remained with me to do this day. It wasn't God who kept walking away. He'd placed his seal on me in childhood and no matter how far I ran from Him, **He remained faithful.** When I finally recognized His unfailing love, I was made free.

2 Timothy 2:13

"If we believe not, yet he abideth faithful: he cannot deny himself."

Ephesians 4:30

"And grieve not the holy Spirit of God, whereby ye are sealed unto the day of redemption."

I let myself be drawn into His loving arms and led by His precious nail-scarred hands. He has kept me securely at His side and taught me important life lessons. Jesus has given me back the freedom I had in Christ on that day when I accepted the precious gift He'd offered. My life in Him is so much fuller than it ever was when I tried to live by the world's standards.

I implore you, if you've known Jesus and strayed, call out to Him.

If you've never know Jesus Christ as your personal Lord and Savior. Find out what it means to have a relationship with Christ. Not religion, but a personal relationship with a loving God.

God makes it clear in His word that there isn't a person righteous enough to get to heaven on their own.

Romans 3:10

"As it is written, There is none righteous, no, not one:"

We are all sinners.

Romans 3:23

For all have sinned, and come short of the glory of God;

Death is the penalty for sin.

Romans 6:23

"For the wages of sin is death; but the gift of God is eternal life through Jesus Christ our Lord."

Christ died on the cross for our sins.

Romans 5:8

"But God commendeth his love toward us, in that, while we were yet sinners, Christ died for us."

If we confess and believe we will be saved.

Romans 10:9

"That if thou shalt confess with thy mouth the Lord Jesus, and shalt believe in thine heart that God hath raised him from the dead, thou shalt be saved."

Once we believe he sets us free.

Romans 8:1

"There is therefore now no condemnation to them which are in Christ Jesus, who walk not after the flesh, but after the Spirit."

I hope you'll take hold of that freedom and start a personal relationship with Christ Jesus.